FOOLISH
EXPECTATIONS

FOOLISH EXPECTATIONS

ALISON BLISS

DEDICATION

Hey, Mom. It's me!
Thank you for all your love and support,
and for encouraging me from the beginning.
Love, Alison…Bliss
(Just in case you forgot who it was.)

Acknowledgements

As ALWAYS, THANK you to my loving husband, Denny, and my amazing boys, Matthew and Andrew, for their never-ending support. I love you guys more than you'll ever know! To my parents, thanks for continuing to be proud of me, even though I write dirty books. Thank you to my mother-in-law, Terry, for loving said dirty books. You have great taste! Much love to my four sisters—Annita, Amanda, April, and Andrea—who, without me, would have to fight to the death to become Dad's favorite.

A big hug to Carol Pavliska for always giving great notes and huge amounts of encouragement. Thank you to Sonya Weiss for your friendship and for being an amazing person. High-five to The Floozies for being such a fun, fierce group of women who always have each other's back, including mine. You ladies are the best!

I couldn't do it all without my amazing PAs: Barbara Campbell, Dana Leah, Crystal Wegrzynowicz (I spelled it right this time!), Cindy Yocum, and Tessa Walters. Huge thanks to the Pure Bliss Street Team, who has always supported me in everything I do. You are all amazing, and I can't imagine going on this journey without you. I have made so many lifelong friends in our group. You guys are unbelievably awesome!

My sincerest gratitude to Gwen Hayes for her brilliant editorial skills and for caring so much about her authors. I adore you, woman! Also, thank you to Judi Weiss for the fabulous copyedits. You are a sweetheart!

I'd like to thank the other authors in The Sutherlands anthology: Robin Covington, Kelly Jamieson, Terri Osburn, Avery Flynn, Abby Niles, Shyla Colt, Julie Particka, Naima

Simone, and Joya Ryan. Never a dull moment with you crazy girls!

And last, but never least, a huge thank you goes out to all the readers, bloggers, and reviewers who have sent so many lovely messages to me and have helped spread the word about my books! I truly believe I have the most awesome fans in the world. You guys are amazing!

CHAPTER ONE

BAILEY HOBBS THOUGHT her day couldn't get any worse. But the moment she stepped inside the small roadside bar in Flat Rock, Texas, she proved herself wrong.

Rowdy's was jam-packed with Stetson-wielding cowboys and not nearly enough women to go around. The men to women ratio was easily twenty to one, and most females in attendance seemed to be already coupled with their picks of lucky bachelors. Which meant every unattached male in the room had looked up, interest gleaming in their eyes, as she'd entered the bar.

It was almost enough to make her turn around and high-tail it back the way she'd come. *Almost.* But sore feet trumped discomforting men any day of the week. And Bailey's feet were killing her. Two long miles in tight, three-inch heels on uneven asphalt had that effect on a girl.

Rowdy's was apparently the place to be on a Saturday night. Not that she'd know, since she never frequented bars, and this was the first time she'd ever wandered into the place. Okay, so limped in was more like it.

She hobbled through the crowd, ignoring the pack of wolf-whistling males who tried to snag her attention as she passed. When she reached a wall of men wearing shit-eating grins and deliberately blocking the aisle ahead of her, Bailey circled toward the bar where she spied a small gap.

A cowboy stood there with his chair pushed back, leaning against the bar with one elbow as he spoke to the bartender. The gap between him and the chair was just large enough for her to slide through. But as she squeezed through the tight space, the man shifted his position, and she ended up rubbing her chest across his back. He stiffened and glanced over his right shoulder, his crystal blue eyes landing on hers. A smile crept onto his lips. Then he seared a laser beam gaze across her chest that would've cut glass. Blatant sexual interest sparked in his eyes, and his tongue darted out, wetting his bottom lip. He gave her a wink and tipped his hat. "Ma'am."

Bailey stood frozen, blinking at him, but she didn't know why.

Her white sheath dress hugged her curves like a second skin, but it only dipped low enough in the front to display a tasteful—*yet apparently mouth-watering*—hint of cleavage. Even still, it wasn't the first time a guy had admired her assets. Hell, she'd just strolled through a wild herd of stallions, chomping at the bit to get her attention, and it hadn't fazed her one bit.

Yet something about the way this man groped her intimately with his eyes had knocked her off balance. His heated look shouldn't have flustered her, but it did. And judging by the way he grinned, he enjoyed *that* way more than the actual rubbing she'd performed on his backside.

"Are you going to stand there blocking the aisle all night, or are you going to move?" The feminine voice had a festering bite, breaking Bailey from her trance-like state.

She turned to find a woman standing behind her, arms crossed, and reeking of liquor. Bailey recognized her. Just moments before, the same girl had been arguing with her boyfriend in the parking lot. And if the scowl was any indication, it hadn't ended well.

"I'm still waiting," the girl rudely noted.

Jeez. Impatient much?

Bailey quickly found her feet and continued on her way, sitting at the only empty table available near the far wall. She glanced back at the bar, but Miss Crankypants had already moved on. The cowboy, however, continued staring at Bailey, studying her from a distance. He smiled, as if he were waiting on an invitation...one he wouldn't receive. At least not from her.

Bailey was in no mood for company. Especially of the male variety. *Been there, done that. Even bought the damn T-shirt.* It was a mental souvenir she'd gladly return if she hadn't lost it somewhere in the shambles of her life. Too bad that wouldn't work—taking a disappointing memory and returning it for a full refund of the emotional purchase price.

She rubbed her throbbing temples. *Yeah, right. If only things were that simple.*

Her life was already chock-full of complicated choices. After the day she'd had, the only decision she felt capable of making was what kind of drink she needed.

First things first, though.

She kicked off her tight-ass shoes and released a sigh of relief. The torturous white pumps with a skinny heel landed somewhere under the table in God knows what, but Bailey didn't care. At least she was off her feet.

She propped her aching bare feet up in the chair across from her, and with a subtle wave of her hand, she flagged down a passing waitress. The tiny woman looked as delicate as a fairy, but flitted around customers with speed and accuracy.

"What can I get for you, sweetie?" the waitress asked, her voice sounding almost as harried as her feet. "Martini or a vodka tonic?"

"How about a beer?"

"Hmm. Didn't see that one coming. In that fancy get-up, you don't seem like the type. Bottle or tap?"

"Bottle."

"My kind of girl." The waitress winked and then moved through the crowd, ducking and dodging until she careened up to the bar.

It dwarfed her and it was arguable whether or not the tiny thing could actually see over the counter. Instead of looking like a waitress fetching a beer, she looked more like a child ordering two scoops of chocolate from an ice cream truck. Only difference was, in here, she was surrounded on both sides by grown men. One of who happened to be the guy with the staring problem.

And it had become chronic.

His body faced the bar, but his neck craned sideways, keeping his intense eyes on her. She hated to admit it, but there was something intriguing—and unnerving—about the way he focused all of his attention on her.

Tufts of dark brown hair peeked out from beneath the back of his black hat and curled at the collar of his gray plaid western shirt. His unshaven five o'clock shadow darkened his jawline, but somehow he still didn't appear to be as rough around the edges as some of the other men in the room. No, actually he stood out. Neatly pressed clothing. Clean, polished snakeskin boots. The expensive-looking gold watch on his left wrist. This guy was no slouch. Oh, he was definitely all male, all right, and—judging from the size of his biceps pressing against his shirt—he looked like the kind of guy who could handle himself in a fight. But she'd bet anything that he was one of those weekend warrior types who didn't shave or style his hair until Monday morning before work.

It was possible he thought the rough appearance made him tougher-looking to the other men in the room. But as far as women went, it didn't matter. This cowboy actually looked more dangerous when he smiled—if that was even possible. *Okay, so he isn't bad-looking.* There, she admitted it. Just because she wasn't interested didn't mean she was blind.

His tight jeans displayed well-muscled thighs and an outstanding ass—two things any woman appreciated on a hot-blooded cowboy. But that didn't mean she had any intention of engaging in innocent flirting. Nothing involving this man would be considered innocent. Indecent, maybe. Probably.

Her gaze continued up his body until it landed on his smiling face. *Oops.* So much for deterring his unwanted attention.

She immediately shifted her eyes and glanced around the room, seeking out other women in the bar. Some spun circles in flouncy skirts and stomped their pink boots on the dance floor, while others sat at tables surrounded on all sides by eager men waiting to ambush them. A few were even being force-fed hard liquor to lower their inhibitions...and probably their standards.

That's when she noticed the rude chick perched at the end of the bar. Like Bailey, she was sitting alone. The young woman tossed back a double shot of something resembling tequila, then held up her finger for another. Undoubtedly, the girl was nursing a broken heart and chasing away her sorrows with alcohol. Sad thing was, she'd most likely end up in the back of a horse trailer later, letting one of these young studs fuck her brains out just to boost her damaged ego.

Bailey's gaze flickered back to her watcher. *Probably someone like him.*

He rose an eyebrow as if he had read her dirty thoughts, and her heart thumped an extra beat. Her stomach twisted into a knot, so she stiffened her posture and turned away. She was trying her best to look disinterested, but somehow kept fumbling up. Hard to ignore someone who refused to ignore you back.

A minute later, the waitress returned and set a beer in front of Bailey, refusing to take the credit card she held out. Instead, the waitress motioned back to the bar. "The gentleman asked me to send his regards."

The smug man tipped his bottle up, took a long pull, and then gave her a quick wink. It didn't surprise Bailey nearly as much as it pissed her off. "Gentleman, my ass. Does that shit really work on the women in here?"

The waitress shrugged. "Apparently."

"Well, I prefer to buy my own beer." Bailey shoved her credit card into the waitress's hand. "Tell Romeo I'm not interested, but the drunk, broken-hearted woman across the bar to his right would make for a decent consolation prize."

The waitress laughed and bumped Bailey with her hip. "Oh, honey, you just made my night! Nash Sutherland has always been too handsome for his own good. You can bet your ass I'm going to relay that message with a smile on my face."

Bailey gave her a terse nod. "Good."

Instead of walking away, though, the waitress leaned closer to her. "Thing is, sweetie, that's probably not going to deter him."

"What, this Nash guy doesn't believe in no meaning no?"

"Oh, nothing like that," the waitress said, shaking her head. "He's a good guy. It's just…well, I don't think he's ever had a

13

woman tell him no before." Then she headed for the bar with the credit card in her hand and a sly grin on her face.

It was only then Bailey realized exactly what the waitress meant. When she approached him and told him the bad news, the gorgeous bastard looked more than a little stunned. He'd obviously expected Bailey to bat her eyelashes and invite him over with a crook of her finger. Because, clearly, that was the way it went for someone like him. Not many women—*if any*—turned him down.

As the waitress continued to speak to him, he glanced over to the depressed, glassy-eyed woman across the bar, then flicked his eyes back to Bailey. His jaw tightened and a coolness took over his face.

Bailey couldn't help but giggle at his reaction. She held up her beer in a casual "cheers" motion, encouraging him to pursue more lucrative ventures…or easier women. But he apparently didn't get the message. If anything, her unintentional taunt had the opposite effect, as if she'd inadvertently issued him a challenge.

A firestorm flashed through his eyes. Definite insult. Mostly anger. Probably a little emasculation. He drained his beer, motioned to the bartender for two more, and grinned like a devil who'd just wagered on her soul.

Shit. Time to go.

Bailey stuffed her sore feet back into her heels, grabbed her purse, and started to stand, but in her hurry, she bumped the table and knocked her beer over. The bottle clanged against the wooden surface as the liquid poured out. *Damn it. What the hell is wrong with me?* The stupid cowboy had flustered her once again. She sat back down, turned the bottle upright, and used the only two bar napkins she had to soak up the mess. It wasn't doing the job.

A few tables over, a young guy jumped up, grabbed a handful of napkins, and offered his assistance. "Here, let me give you a hand."

"Thanks," she said, sopping up the last of it. "I spilled a whole beer."

"That's all right. I already ordered you another," he said just as the waitress appeared next to him with another round of drinks.

"Oh, no. That's okay. I was just leaving."

He paid and tipped the waitress, then set the beer down in front of Bailey with a persistent clunk. "No need to rush off." He grabbed a chair, turned it around, and sat on it backward next to her, blocking the only escape route she had. "We've barely gotten to know each other. At least drink the beer I bought before you go. You don't want to waste another one, do ya?"

"Sorry. I appreciate it, I do. But I have to work in the morning," she said, rising from her chair.

The man grabbed her hand and tugged her back into place. "Aw, come on. You can't leave yet. I didn't even get a chance to ask you your name." His calloused hand landed firmly on her knee.

She tensed. "It's…uh, Sheila, but I really should—"

"Pretty name for such a pretty lady." His hand quickly worked its way up her bare thigh.

She tensed and pushed his hand off her, but before she could say anything, someone kicked the guy's chair with enough force to jar his entire body. Both of them looked up to see the man named Nash standing beside the other man's chair, holding a beer in each hand. "Might want to put your hands on someone else's woman if you want to keep them."

"Aw, damn you, Nash!" The guy rose from his chair and shook his head. "You got dibs on this one?"

Nash nodded. "I do."

"Man, I'm gonna have to find a new hangout if I want a fighting chance at getting some decent puss—"

"I wouldn't finish that sentence if I were you." A vein throbbed in Nash's temple and his fingers tightened their grip on the bottles he held. "In fact, you better start looking now before I knock all the teeth out of that foul mouth of yours."

The man threw his hands up in surrender. "Whoa! Okay, okay, I'm going," the coward said, backing away slowly until he was in the clear. Then he went to find someone else to molest. *Thank Goodness.*

This time, Nash didn't wait for an invitation. He pulled the empty chair back around to the other side of the table, turned it around, and sat across from Bailey, sliding her a beer. "You okay, sweetheart?"

She crossed her arms and blew out a hard breath. "I don't believe I sent up any smoke signals, Chief."

He grinned slyly. "Don't need to now, sweetheart. I marked you as my woman. He won't bother you again, and he'll spread the word to the rest of them."

Stunned by that revelation, she looked around the bar and, sure enough, there were several men glancing over and pointing in her direction. "So you...placed a *claim* on me?"

"Just for tonight. But don't worry, it was for a good cause. Richard's a scum-bag with a reputation for getting grabby with the ladies."

Of course the molester's name is Richard. Figures.

She rolled her eyes. "Yeah, I already had the overwhelming pleasure of that experience."

"Well, Sheila," he said with a wink. "You don't have to worry about that idiot anymore. Not with me here."

Christ, he thought her name was Sheila! She smiled at that. Oh well, no point in correcting him. *Shouldn't believe everything you overhear, buddy.* "You mean, because he wouldn't take no for an answer?"

"Yep. Exactly."

Bailey leaned toward him and rested her elbows on the table. "So, tell me...Nash, is it?" she asked sweetly. "Tell me how I should handle a persistent man with a blatant disregard for the word *no*."

"Ah, hell, darlin'. Most women can get away with a polite rejection," he said easily. "But if that doesn't work, then something a little more volatile is sometimes needed." He leaned back in his chair and tipped the bottle to his lips. "That's where I come in."

"Good thing you were here, then."

He nodded. "Sure was."

"I guess I should thank you."

"Yep." He took another swig of his beer.

Bailey stood up so quickly, her chair banged against the wall and the entire bar came to a standstill. She slapped both hands on the table in front of her and glared at him. "Thank you, then…you egotistical jerk!"

Nash choked on his beer. "Wait. What?"

"Thanks for wasting ten minutes of my life I'll never get back. If I had wanted to have this pointless conversation with you, I'd have invited you over here myself. But since I didn't, you decided to prove what a stud you are."

He shook his head. "Now, wait just a damn min—"

"Isn't that what you are around here—the Thoroughbred stallion running fast and free with all the loose fillies?"

He looked unsure how to respond. "I…uh…"

"Well, I hate to screw up your breeding plans, Bucko, but you can get lost. This filly has nothing to offer you." As if the cocky sonofabitch couldn't help himself, his gaze lowered, pissing her off more. "Stop staring at my boobs. I didn't dress this way for you. In fact, let's get something else straight. I'm not your darlin', your sweetheart, or some drunk chick you can persuade into going home with you."

He peered around and seemed to realize everyone in the bar was staring at them. His expression hardened. "You done yelling at me yet?"

Breathing a little harder than before, Bailey composed herself and smoothed out her dress. "If you men wouldn't dangle your manhood out there for everyone to see, then you wouldn't have to worry about some woman wrapping her teeth around it."

Nash stared at her for a moment, then smirked. "Was that an offer?"

A couple of men playing pool nearby chuckled.

"Jesus. You're impossible." She grabbed her purse and stormed out.

CHAPTER TWO

NASH SUTHERLAND SHOOK his head.

Hell, all he had done was buy her a beer and rescue her from some pervert with his hand halfway up her skirt. If she'd wanted to verbally assault someone, that dickhead should've been the one on the receiving end. But, no. She'd yelled at him instead. Publicly. Like *he* was the pervert. The little blonde spitfire had unleashed her fury on the wrong man.

Sure, for a brief moment, he might have wondered how soft the inside of her thighs were and how they'd respond to his tongue trailing up them into parts unknown. But it wasn't like he'd done it.

Nash might have come on a little strong and pushed his way over to her table, even after she'd declined the beer he'd tried to buy her, but he would never have forced himself on her like that shit-for-brains had. And after the way she'd yelled at him, Nash had been inclined to let her storm off. *Insane-ass woman.*

But seconds after the angry blonde disappeared out the front door, he caught sight of Richard slipping out a side exit with a sinister grin on his face.

Fuck.

The girl obviously didn't want company—his or anyone else's, for that matter—but she was damn sure going to get it, whether she liked it or not. Nash jumped out of his chair and went after her.

She made it to the parking lot before he caught her. His hand shot out and latched onto her wrist, turning her around. "Wait a minute."

"Let go of me."

When she jerked her arm, he tightened his grip. He didn't see Richard anywhere, but he wasn't about to let her keep walking farther away from the safety of the bar...or him. "Hold on. I need to talk to you."

She tried to wrench herself loose, but he held on. Out of frustration, she swung at him with her free arm. All he could do was keep a tight hold on her and block her flailing limbs. "Damn it! What's your problem, lady?"

She gritted her teeth. "I asked you to let go of me."

"No, you didn't. You ordered me to. Look, I'm not going to hurt you. I just need to tell you something."

"I don't have to listen to anything, you stupid asshole."

This time, she swung her purse, clocking him in the cheek before he could duck. And then, as if being bitch-slapped with a brick wasn't bad enough, the enraged woman tried to kick him in the nuts...and actually grazed one of them.

Sonofabitch.

Nash maneuvered her back against the tailgate of a nearby pickup. He took it easy on her, but he also had to protect himself until she calmed down. Both of them were already breathing heavy. "Are you done trying to kick my ass yet?"

She glared at him, fire burning in her eyes. "Are you so hard up for a woman that you have to chase one into the parking lot because you can't accept that she refused your advances?"

"Sweetheart, I haven't even begun to make advances on you. If I had, we'd be in my bed screwing instead of standing in this parking lot." He blocked her attempt at hitting him again and chuckled softly at her indignation. "Would you stop hitting me already? I told you I wasn't going to hurt you. I only came out to make sure—"

"God, you really think you're something special, don't you?"

Well, I am a Sutherland...

He rolled his eyes at the thought. That was exactly the way his father looked at things, not Nash. He had more respect and pride in himself than that.

Aaron Sutherland wielded the power of the family name and flaunted their fortune every chance he got. But Nash didn't want anything to do with it. As far as he was concerned, his father could take his inheritance and shove it up his ass...which was exactly what he'd told him the last time they'd spoken. *The prick.*

"I don't think any such thing," Nash said, scoffing at her remark.

"Oh, really? Well, why else would you come all the way out here to give me one last chance to sleep with you?"

That's what she thought I was doing? Christ.

He sighed. "You have it all wrong. I came out here only to make sure you were okay." He released her and backed away to make sure she understood he was no threat. "You were being followed...by someone other than me."

She stilled and her eyes widened. "What are you talking about?"

The sound of the country music grew louder and they both looked up to see Richard slipping through the front door, heading back inside the bar. Nash glanced back at her to make sure she fully understood the situation.

Momentarily stunned, a soft little "oh" whispered past her parted lips. Her eyes glazed over, but it wasn't anger he saw there. It was something different, something that grabbed his attention and held on tight. Fear.

"I...I only wanted a beer," she said, her voice trembling. "Just a cold beer." Tears welled up in her eyes. "But apparently wearing a stupid dress in that bar declares hunting season officially open with me as the big game trophy." Sniffling, she wiped away a stray tear with the back of her hand. "And believe me, I didn't come here with any intention of being mounted or stuffed."

Silently, he stared at her for a full minute. Then he pushed himself off the tailgate and stepped back, shoving his hand in his right pocket. He pulled out his keys and motioned with his head. "Come on."

She stood there dumbfounded, twisting her fingers together, as he crossed the parking lot and climbed into his gold Chevy truck. She hadn't moved a muscle, so he started the engine and shifted into reverse, backing across the parking lot until the truck was even with her. He motored down the window. "You coming?"

She glanced down at her feet, then shifted uncomfortably. "I, uh...where are we going?"

"You said you wanted a cold beer. I know just the place."

Her gaze met his once again, but her blue eyes had dulled to an ashy gray as if her confidence had diminished. He hated that. Nash wanted to see that fiery spark she'd had when she'd let him have it in the bar. So he added, "You want it or not?" He grinned sinfully and arched one brow, knowing it came off as a double entendre.

She scoffed at his remark. "Yeah, I want it. The beer, I mean."

Nash grinned as she opened the door and lifted her leg to climb inside...until the hem of her dress inched upward and stretched tight across her slender thighs. He blew out a slow breath and nonchalantly adjusted himself, hoping to alleviate the uncomfortable crowding going on in his jeans. But as she slid into the seat, closed the door, and turned to grab the seat belt, her skirt only rose higher.

He gripped the steering wheel harder, forcing himself to keep his eyes on the road as he drove out of the parking lot.

"So, do you want to tell me why I deserved the public humiliation you unleashed on me back there?"

She grimaced. "Look, I've had a rough day, okay? I'm sorry if I took it out on you, but I don't want to talk about it."

"Okay, fair enough. Where are you from?"

"How about we just forget the talking altogether?"

"It's a simple question."

She stared out the passenger window and sighed. "Here."

"Here, as in Flat Rock?"

"No, here as in the mesquite tree we just passed," she said, her tone ringing with sarcasm. "Of course I meant Flat Rock. What kind of question is that?"

Her sharp words came out almost hateful, littered with an untrusting, smart-ass zing, but he recognized the attitude for what it was. Someone had done something to get this energetic young woman's back up, and Nash would bet almost anything that someone had been a man. Judging by the ugly scowl on her pretty face, she'd had just about enough of them.

"Houston isn't far away, you know. Or you could have been from any of the surrounding cities. Flat Rock isn't all that big compared to most places, yet I've never seen you around town."

"There's fifteen thousand residents in Flat Rock. I doubt you know the other fourteen thousand nine hundred ninety-eight of them. Or did you pick them all up in a bar, too?"

He grinned. "Well, I can see conversation comes naturally to you." Then he leveled a sardonic gaze at her and shook his head. "Why don't you relax a little? I'm not the bad guy here."

"*That* has yet to be determined," she said coolly.

Nash thought about that for a moment. "Want me to prove it?"

"How? You going to put on your 'I'm not the bad guy' badge?" Her smile teetered between irritation and amusement. "Or maybe you're going to show me the superhero leotard under your clothes? Is that it—you've got your spidey-roos on?"

He shook his head. *Christ, she's a smart-ass.* A long-legged, sexy smart-ass with a sharp tongue and a curvy little body that he wanted pressed against his. "I have something a little different in mind, but I think it'll convince you."

"I doubt it."

He shrugged and turned right on the next street. "Nothing more fun than proving someone wrong."

A few minutes later, they veered onto a long caliche-paved driveway and followed it up to a red brick ranch-style home, complete with an old wooden barn and fenced pastures. Several curious horses lifted their heads at the sound of the approaching truck. Nash pulled up in front of the house and shut off the engine.

She glanced around warily. "I…I thought you were taking me to a bar?"

"Sweetheart, there's not a bar in this city you can go into wearing a dress like that and *not* get hit on by some idiot. You're safer having a drink here."

"Where's *here?*"

"My house," he said, smiling at the panic that flashed across her face. "Calm down. It's not what you think."

"Oh, really?" The panic quickly changed to irritation. "Like you even have a clue as to what I'm thinking?"

He leaned his arm on the steering wheel and looked directly into her eyes. "You're thinking I brought you here with the intention of putting the moves on you so I could get you into bed.

You're wrong. I brought you here to show you I can be a gentleman."

"Okay, so let me get this straight. You're proving that you're a gentleman by taking me home with you?" She shook her head. "You're fucking delusional."

"No, I'm going to prove it by keeping my hands to myself."

"Right. And I'm supposed to believe that?"

Nash tried to be patient with her, but didn't appreciate being treated like he was some kind of predator. "I don't know what kind of men you're used to hanging out with, but I would never touch a woman in a sexual manner unless she asked me to. So unless you give me a green light, you're perfectly safe with me."

"Oh, trust me, I won't."

"Then I reckon you have nothing to worry about," he said, hoping his sincerity registered in his tone. She still didn't look convinced, though. "Okay, fine. Tell me where you live and I'll take you home."

He moved to start the engine, but she placed her hand on his arm. "Um, Nash…wait." Their eyes met briefly, and she bit her lip. "I didn't get the beer you promised me."

Nash nodded and climbed out of the truck, wiping the grin off his face before he sauntered around to the front bumper where she met him. They strolled side-by-side up to the front porch together, where he unlocked the door and reached inside to flip on the lights before they entered.

He left her standing near the front door while he stepped in the kitchen and grabbed two beers from the fridge. He twisted the lids off on his way back to her and tossed them on the coffee table. When he handed her a beer, she fumbled it a little, demonstrating how nervous she was. Probably wasn't sure if she had let her guard down or if he had simply changed tactics. Either way, though, she'd ended up in his living room with a beer in her hand.

Damn, I'm better than I thought.

Nash plopped down on the couch, but she stayed standing, uncomfortably shifting her weight from one foot to the other. "You don't have to stand by the door," he said, motioning to the couch. "I promise I won't bite."

"I'm fine." She shifted her weight again and gazed at the rodeo trophies on the bookshelf. "Is this what you do for a living?"

"No, I own a law practice. I retired from the rodeo circuit when I was younger, after cracking every rib in my body and getting kicked in the head one too many times." He watched her squirm painfully in one place. She was itching to kick off those fucking shoes, just like she'd done at the bar and again in his truck. But she probably thought doing so in an intimate setting would translate as some sort of invitation.

Nash sighed. "Sweetheart, you can sit down. I'm not going to pull a Richard."

She grinned at that, but continued to stand by the door. "It's okay," she said, shifting her weight again. "I'm fine."

"Oh, for Pete's sake." He stood, walked over, and pulled the beer out of her hand, placing it on a nearby bookshelf, then scooped her off her feet.

She shrieked as he walked several feet, and tossed her onto the couch. When he placed his hand on her knee, she practically crab-crawled up the wall to get away from him. "What the hell do you think you're doing?"

"Jesus. Calm down. I'm only taking these off." Frowning, he reached down and pulled both of her shoes loose, holding them up for her to see. "These are stupid shoes. Anyone can see that they hurt your feet. Do yourself a favor and buy boots or sneakers next time."

He tossed the white torture devices on the floor and sat down on the couch, lifting both of her feet into his lap. She tensed and pulled away, but he firmed his grip and started massaging, pressing hard into the ball of her foot. He made slow, circular motions with his thumbs and kneaded at the tension in her tired feet.

A small sigh of pleasure escaped her lips as her body relaxed and she melted under his touch. His hands stilled momentarily, then resumed. That little sweet moan had hit a nerve, and the large bulge in his pants confirmed it. He manipulated her feet, but this woman was screwing with his head...both of them. Because although he'd promised not to touch her in a sexual way, her feet were now resting comfortably on his prominent boner, one she clearly was aware of.

The tension in the room thickened and her cheeks blushed fiercely. "Okay, you can stop now," she said softly. He ignored her and kept rubbing. "No, really. Thank you, but my feet feel much better."

"Problem?"

"No, I…" She blew out a breath. "Well, it's just that…"

"Go on," he said, grinning.

"Okay, so you obviously want me to say it out loud." She wouldn't look at him, and her cheeks glowed more brilliantly with heat. Without a doubt, she didn't want to openly discuss his raging hard-on. So instead, she looked back at him and blurted out, "Your hands are rough."

He laughed. "Chicken."

"Fine. Is there anything that *doesn't* turn you on?"

"Yeah," he said, measuring her carefully with his eyes. "Consolation prizes."

CHAPTER THREE

BAILEY GIGGLED. "STILL mad about that, huh? Hey, she was attractive in that drunken mean girl kind of way. Probably not the worst you could do."

"I know you may not believe this, but I don't settle. Ever." He leveled a gaze at her that made her heart skip a beat. "Or take advantage of wounded women."

Sure you do. You just don't know it yet.

The moment Nash had offered to take her home, she'd had no choice but to change her tune. She didn't want to admit she had nowhere to go. Her apartment was gone, her things had already been moved out, and even her cell phone was missing in action. She couldn't afford to stay in a hotel, and even if she could, she didn't want to explain to Nash why she would need to.

Oh, hell. Who am I kidding? That wasn't the only reason she'd changed her mind and she knew it.

Nash had proven he was a decent guy…even if he was a bit cocky for her taste. Not only had he saved her from Richard—twice—but he'd offered to do the noble thing and take her home rather than push her to come inside.

After what she'd been through earlier tonight, her opinion of men was at an all-time low. So it was almost comical that she would cross paths with a guy who wore his white knight complex like a badge of honor. It was definitely an attractive quality.

Up to this point, she'd done well enough keeping her fluctuating hormones hidden under a cloak of sarcasm. But with his overt sexual nature, she wasn't sure she could keep it up much longer. Maybe it was best not to contemplate what undoubtedly would happen if she gave him a chance to make his big play. *No, no, no. If I'm smart, I'll get the hell out of Dodge before he does just that.*

With very little effort, the man already had her lying on his couch, moaning with pleasure. And she still had her clothes on. If she stayed much longer, she'd be naked and under him and getting a hell of a lot more than a foot rub. She just needed a moment to think.

She pushed her wavy blonde hair off her shoulders, and with a slight touch, trailed her fingers slowly across her lips, contemplating what to do. It was a nervous habit, but she never realized how sensuous and feminine it could be until she caught him watching her do it. His gaze shot back and forth, as if his eyes couldn't decide between her mouth and her chest.

"Stop looking at my breasts."

He gave her a sexy little smile. "Would you prefer I touch them?"

Something low and deep moved through her, but she wasn't about to tell him that. His womanizing attitude pissed her off. She hadn't meant to get so upset in the bar, but it wasn't like the arrogant ass hadn't deserved it. She guessed that the jabs she'd made at his male ego were what had him so frustrated. "It must break your heart that I'm not falling over myself to tear your clothes off."

Judging by the irritation on his face, she'd guessed right. That's exactly what had him so worked up. He couldn't understand why a woman—*any woman*—didn't want him rammed eight inches inside her. She moved her foot subtly. *Or was it nine?*

"Not really. But if you decide you want to do more than play footsie with my cock, I can have that dress off and my dick inside you in three seconds flat."

A pulse of heat throbbed between her legs, and she squeezed them together to relieve the ache. He gave her a sly grin, knowing full well the reaction he had caused. Apparently, sexual banter was foreplay to him.

"You know, you didn't like it when that Richard creep made a derogatory comment in front of me."

"At that point, you were still a lady who was as pretty as a rose."

"And that somehow changed?"

"Yeah, I forgot roses have thorns." He lifted a brow. "What's with you, anyway? You're not nearly as shocked and offended by the vulgarities as you pretend to be."

"Maybe I am."

He chuckled, shaking his head. "Sweetheart, I've ridden bulls tamer than you. You should just be glad I like feisty women."

She rolled her eyes. "I can hardly contain the joy."

"Oh, come on," he groaned. "I thought we'd pulled that stick out of your ass a while ago. Here I was thinking we'd end the night with a bang."

Of course he did. Because that's all men wanted. *Damn it.* Anger stabbed through her, sharp and hot, and Bailey jumped off the couch, snatched her apparently-stupid shoes from the floor, and headed for the front door. She was an idiot for letting down her guard with him.

"What's wrong with you?" he asked coming up behind her, confusion tainting his voice.

She whirled on him. "You are! All you men are!"

He looked around, as if he was expecting to see another person in the room. "What men? What the hell are you talking about?"

"God, I'm so dumb." She bounced around on one foot, trying to put her shoe on. "Here I was starting to think you were a nice guy, and you couldn't help yourself. You just had to prove me wrong."

"Want to clue me in on what I did?"

"Like you don't know?" She pressed her other shoe hard into his chest. "You men think with your dicks. All because you're not man enough to be with one woman."

Nash narrowed his eyes, but didn't speak.

Bailey cocked her head. "What? Low blow?"

"I'd say it was a shot below the belt. Just wish I knew what I did to deserve it."

"Jesus. You aren't even listening." Holding one shoe, she limped toward the front door. "Forget it. Go back to the bar and find some other pathetic girl who'll end your night with a *bang*."

She started to open it, but his hand shoved it closed. "Wait a minute."

"I don't have anything else to say to you."

"Good, then you'll shut up and listen." She opened her mouth to speak, but he raised his hand to stop her. "You misunderstood me. I didn't mean it the way it sounded. It's just an expression, one I'll admit I used carelessly. I'm sorry."

"Fine. Apology accepted. Goodbye." She tried to open the door again, but he put his hand on it.

"One more thing," he said, glaring at her. "Where the hell do you get off telling me what I'm man enough for? I'll have you know, I've dated plenty of women exclusively, and I've never cheated on a single one. I've never claimed to be a saint, but I'm not the devil you're portraying me as, either. I don't go to bars to pick up stray women any more than I go there to pick up stray men. That doesn't mean I haven't ever gone home with one."

Her eyes widened.

"*Women*, damn it! I'm talking about women." Nash took off his cowboy hat, tossed it on the coffee table, and then ran his fingers through his unkempt hair.

Bailey covered her mouth, but the giggle leaked out, anyway.

His jaw set and his brows hunched over his eyes. He wasn't amused. "I don't get you," he said, shaking his head. "Hell, I don't even know why I half-ass like you."

She grinned at his frustration. Because, damn it, she half-ass liked him, too. "You said I was…spunky? Wasn't that the word you used?"

"Cheerleaders are spunky. I said you were feisty, like a wiry little kitten ready to dig her claws into someone."

"You didn't say that last part earlier."

He shrugged. "So I summarized a bit. Sue me." He grabbed her beer off the nearby bookshelf, downed half of it, and held the bottle out for her to take.

But she didn't accept it. She was too distracted by his deep blue eyes to move. Every part of this man was aesthetically pleasing, but his intense eyes were something else. Like when he looked at her, he probed her in intimate places. She was so lost in his gaze she barely noticed her trembling fingers had moved to her lips.

He set the bottle down and came closer, heightening her awareness of him. "You know, when I first saw those pouty lips of yours, I couldn't wait to hear your voice. I wondered if it would be as smooth and silky as those long, sexy legs of yours." He rubbed the back of his hand gently over her cheek.

Oh, no. Panicking, she quickly lowered her head and sighed. "Nash, we shouldn't... I mean, it isn't right."

"Probably not. But you're driving me crazy with your give-'em-hell attitude and the way you touch your lips when you're nervous." He lifted her chin and moved closer to her. "Maybe this is only a temporary solution to a permanent problem, but..." His mouth grazed her jawline until his lips reached her ear. "I want to fuck you."

Every muscle in her body clenched tight as she blinked in shock. It wasn't his crude words. Or his intentions. It was the internal revelation that she wanted him to do just that. He pulled back and waited patiently for her answer, but Bailey couldn't look at him any longer. The sexy, come hither look he wore had her heart leaping hurdles in her chest. He wanted to fuck her brains out and—*my God*—she wanted him to. *Holy hell. I'm the girl in the horse trailer!*

"Say something," he pleaded, his rough voice growing huskier, sexier.

She walked several steps away, thinking, considering, agonizing over the decision. It wasn't right, she knew that. But she'd held out this long and that hadn't made her want it any less. Chances were good that she would regret this tomorrow, but for tonight, she wanted to unleash the desire she'd held onto so tightly.

After another moment of hesitation, she reached up behind her and unzipped the back of her dress. Shivers wracked her body as the cool air washed over her skin. Or maybe it was from the anticipation of his touch.

He stepped up behind her, pressing his hard chest into her back as his warm breath caressed her neck. "Sweetheart, I'm not going to decipher messages. I made you a promise, one I intend to keep. If you want me to touch you, you're going to have to say so."

She didn't turn around. "I thought you said you were a lawyer?"

"I am."

"Then you should know better than anyone," she whispered, trying to keep her voice from trembling. "Never stop at a green light."

Even through their clothing, she felt his cock jerk against her ass. Nash pressed his large hands against her back and slowly parted her dress. It fell off her shoulders and down her arms, exposing the white lacy push-up bra and rounded mounds of her breasts. Not pausing for a moment, he lithely unfastened her bra, letting it fall away as his rough fingers glided under her arms and around her ribs. He palmed her, lifting both breasts and weighing them in his cupped hands.

When his fingertips began to tease her nipples, she closed her eyes and reveled in the new sensations he created. She reached back with her left hand, running her fingers up his neck and into his hair, as he pressed firmly into her from behind. Her other hand searched for stability in the form of his belt loop, and she linked her finger through it to keep from floating away.

He kissed down her neck, then nibbled his way back up. Goose bumps broke out on every limb as his hand trailed downward, dove under the front of her dress, and then traced back up her bare thigh until he found her. He cupped her, then probed one finger under the edge of her satin panties. Breathlessly, she moved against him, desire consuming her until she became dizzy from the lack of oxygen in her brain.

But he stopped and pulled away. Confusion and embarrassment barely had time to register before his hands were on her again, his quick fingers peeling her dress down her hips. He dropped it to the floor before hooking onto her panties and stripping her of those, too. She hadn't even kissed him, yet she stood in front of him, with the lights on, completely nude while he was still fully clothed.

Oh God.

But it was too late to be bashful.

Taking her hand, he led her down the hall to his moonlit bedroom and stared indecently at her naked flesh while pulling off his own shirt and kicking off his boots. He steered her over to the bed and shoved her backward with a gentle playfulness in his eyes and a smile on his face. Then he covered her body and mouth with his.

The kiss was neither friendly, nor polite. His tongue parted her lips and swept inside, making her tremble beneath him. He ravaged her mouth with the confidence of a highly skilled lover, leaving her breathless as she desperately groped his back for more of him. Then he nibbled her bottom lip before slowly licking and kissing his way down her stomach to a more intimate area.

She hadn't expected it and froze.

Like a tidal wave, a cascade of sensations rushed forward, sweeping her up in a whirlpool of hypnotic swirls. The vortex pulled at her, sucking her in deeper and deeper until she could no longer catch her breath. No doubt she'd drown before she reappeared at the surface. *Too much, too fast.*

She hadn't moved a single muscle, but suddenly found herself pushing at his shoulders, hindering Nash until he stopped. "What's wrong, baby? Why'd you stop me?"

"Can we just…move on? You know, get this part over with? I…um, don't know how much more I can take."

He glowered at her. "Jesus. You make it sound like I'm performing a root canal on you." He stood up fast, so fast she thought he was calling the whole thing off. But instead, he discarded his pants while grumbling under his breath. "You know, if we're going to have sex, you might actually want to try enjoying it."

She could've died of embarrassment. Christ, she wanted to. Instead, she lay there staring at the ceiling. The crinkling sound of a foil wrapper assured her he was arming them against diseases, which made her breathe a sigh of relief.

At least one of us came prepared.

Crawling up her body, he quickly spread her trembling legs with his. He held himself over her, made a few adjustments down below, and roughly burrowed himself into her.

She gasped.

The searing heat sobered her, but the intense throbbing depleted her of life-sustaining oxygen. Never in her life had she

32

become sweaty and short of breath in three seconds flat. Until now. But it was too late to do anything about it. They formed a tight bond of warm flesh after one forceful stroke had not only detected her virginity, but plowed right through it.

She'd convinced herself he wouldn't notice. That she wouldn't have to explain anything. But Nash grunted and stilled himself above Bailey with a worried look that probably matched her own. Undoubtedly, both of them realized the impact of a well-equipped man having full-on intercourse with a virgin. Her lesson came in the form of pain and embarrassment, but his came with what looked like heightened pleasure…and apparently anger.

CHAPTER FOUR

SONOFABITCH. NASH MUTTERED a few more expletives out loud. "Christ. I didn't know you were a—"

"I don't want to talk about it. I just want to finish this." Her eyes glazed with tears.

"No," he said, shaking his head. "Not like this." He started to ease away from her, but she wrapped her legs around his hips to stop him. The clenching of her tight channel around him made him brace himself by digging his fingers into her hips as he groaned with sensitivity. "Jesus. Stay still."

"Please, don't stop."

"Goddamnit, I have to. As tight as you are, I'm not going to last long. And this isn't fair to you. If I had known—"

"It doesn't matter now. I'm technically not a virgin anymore. Just finish it. Please, Nash. I want you to." Her eyes pleaded with him. "I…I *need* you to."

The desperation in her voice called to him, but his eyes held hers. "You'll regret this in the morning."

"Then let me worry about that," she said, shifting once again.

Fuck. He closed his eyes to keep them from rolling into the back of his head. Holding himself entirely still, he let out a long, slow breath, allowing himself to recover from the overwhelming sensations threatening his control.

He knew he should back off and tell her to find another guy. But the need to protect her from the Richards of the world was enough to keep him from doing so. And, if he were being honest, the thought of another man's dick between her legs pissed him the fuck off. "Fine. But if we're going to do this, then we do it *my* way. It has to be good for you, too. Either that, or we stop now."

Her eyebrow rose. "Okay, what's *your* way?"

Nash grinned, then gently spread her legs wider and slipped his hand in between them. He was still rock hard inside her, but he didn't dare move. Instead, he massaged her clit, squeezing it gently between his fingers while he listened to her breath hitching with every delicate touch. He'd only meant to heighten her pleasure and reduce the pain his intrusion had caused, but he found himself breathing heavier and holding himself painfully back.

God, she's so fucking tight.

She squirmed in response to the extra attention while his own divine patience seared him from the inside out. Every mewling sound she made had him fighting the urge to move inside her. But instead, he continued using the direct touch of his fingers on her clit to counteract the discomfort of him filling her. No matter what, her needs came first.

He waited until her body was damn near vibrating before he began to slowly thrust his hips, gently angling his body and rocking into her with a rhythmic motion. When he pinpointed a sensitive area that had her body jolting, she closed her eyes and held her breath. Oh, fuck yeah. She was getting close.

"Uh-uh, keep them open. I want to see your eyes when you let go."

She opened them and gazed up at him in despair. "I…feel like…like I'm going to spontaneously combust."

Christ. She's never even had an orgasm before. "That's the idea," he whispered, watching her face as she ventured closer to the threshold.

Panic flashed in her eyes. "No, wait. I can't…breathe."

"It's okay, baby. Don't fight it. Just let it happen. It'll feel good, I promise."

One of her hands clutched at the blanket frantically, while the other flew to her mouth. She rubbed at her lips nervously, and he about lost it. Sensations he'd never felt before radiated through him as the heated urgency took over. What the fuck was it about this girl? Dear God, he couldn't get enough of her.

His strong thrusts became more demanding while he again tried to keep his eyes from rolling into the back of his head. Her eyes, on the other hand, were like the ocean, where the color darkens the deeper you get. Wild hunger lingered beneath the surface, fueled by the mind-blowing sexual tension her body created as it gripped him tighter and tighter, as if she were tugging at his very soul.

Finally, she succumbed, biting her fist to muffle the scream she released. With a delighted grin, he stroked more primitively into her as the contractions seized both of their bodies. Nash matched her quivering reflexes and grunted with the exertion of his own feverish climax.

Holy shit. He'd never come so hard before in his life.

They hovered together, gasping in large, heavy breaths as their heart rates returned to normal. She gazed up at him with an adorable, dazed, cartoonish look. But it was Nash who felt like he'd just had an anvil dropped on his head.

He'd slept with his fair share of women in the past. So why the hell had this time been so different? It was as if the intimacy they'd shared matched nothing Nash had ever experienced before.

Only moments ago, she had been untouched, but now... He'd somehow branded her, searing her with his mark. *Mine.* The thought crashed through him with such force, he didn't know what to think. Somehow, it was like she belonged in his bed…with him inside her.

He'd never really believed in love at first sight, but this damn sure wasn't just lust he was feeling. Something about this woman called to him. Like she'd grabbed him by the balls and wouldn't let go.

As he reluctantly separated from her, she smiled, and satisfaction swelled his chest. Nothing could ruin this moment between them. Nothing.

Then he looked down. "Oh, shit." His eyes shot back up to hers. "The sonofabitch broke."

Her eyes widened, and she sat up in a panic. "Oh, my God! I broke your—"

"No, not *that*…the condom. Don't you think I'd be a little more concerned if you broke my dick?"

It was as if her relief morphed into irritation. "Well, I don't know why you're yelling at *me*. If it was an operator error, then that's on you. I never touched it…well, technically."

He gave her a "yeah, right" look, and then eased her out of the bed. They stopped at a trash can before he maneuvered her into the connecting bathroom and ushered her into the shower. She must've thought he was letting her go first because she squeaked a little when he stepped into the stall behind her.

Obviously, the woman had never showered with anyone before. And if her silence was any indication, she wasn't sure of the rules. Not that there *were* any rules. But if she wasn't talking, then neither was he.

Maybe she was preoccupied with the problem at hand. Or maybe she was disappointed with him and the things he… No, that definitely wasn't it. He'd seen the way she'd unraveled beneath him. No woman could fake an orgasm that strong even on her best day. Either way, he wasn't going to ask. At least not yet.

They showered in silence, then rinsed and dried off. She wrapped a towel around herself, refusing to let her eyes meet his, and headed into the bedroom before him. Actually, she hadn't looked at him at all since they'd gotten out of bed. It frustrated him that he wasn't sure what she was thinking, and he needed to do something about it before things between them went even further south.

He slung a towel around his waist and headed into the bedroom to find her. She'd retrieved her clothes from the living room and was sitting on the edge of the bed, holding them in her hands.

"Sorry I shut down in there," he said, gauging her reaction. "I've just never gone…uh, skydiving without a parachute before. This is a first for me."

She trembled, looking timid and fragile, but didn't lift her eyes. "Same here."

Ah, shit. He ran his fingers through his damp hair. "I'm sorry if I'm being a jerk. It was your first time for…well, everything. You're probably scared to death, while I'm over here belly-aching." When she didn't respond, he lifted her chin with his finger. "Are you okay? I mean, physically? I didn't hurt you too much, did I?"

"I'm fine." But her words sounded weak and unsure as her voice cracked from the emotion welling up inside her throat.

"Are you upset with me, then?"

"No." She sniffled a little. "I'm just being stupid and sentimental. I'd always thought my first time would be with my husband on our wedding night, not…a stranger who I'd just met."

Nash sighed heavily. "Damn it. I knew you'd regret it. I just didn't think it would be this soon."

"Oh, no," she said, shaking her head. "That's not what I meant. Nash, I *don't* regret it one bit."

He wanted to grin but thought that might be the equivalent of high-fiving his dick. So instead, he sat down beside her and pressed his lips to her temple. "Are you worried about the condom mishap?"

"As far as pregnancy goes? No. I don't think so. I'm pretty sure the timing is off." She glanced over at him, but he knew he didn't look any more relieved than she did. "Should I be…concerned, though?" she asked, cringing at her own words.

Without spelling it out, he knew exactly what she meant. "I've been tested," he admitted. "Unless you're a needle junkie or something, then you're clean, too. Pregnancy is probably our only real concern. I'd want to know if you were, but since you don't think you are…"

"We dodged a bullet, then?"

He shrugged. "I'd say so."

She gave him an awkward smile and sighed. "Well, I guess it's time for me to get dressed and go—"

"No. Why don't you stay here tonight? I'll take you home in the morning."

She blinked rapidly, probably wondering if she'd heard him right. But Nash never thought of himself as a wham-bam kind of man. *Not usually, anyway.*

"I don't have anything to sleep in."

He grinned and loosened the knot in her towel over her breasts. "Doesn't matter. You won't need it."

CHAPTER FIVE

BAILEY AWOKE TO warm fingers trailing down her stomach to her nether regions. She slapped at his hands and rolled away. "Get away from me, you creep!"

"What?" Nash laughed and reached for her again. "I thought you said you liked it?"

"That's before I knew you were as unstable as an old stick of dynamite. Don't you have to recharge or something? You know, come up to the surface for a breath?"

"Oh, come on, sweetheart. I'll even let you light the fuse this time. In fact, if we create enough friction, I'll guarantee sparks." He winked at her.

She smirked, knowing full-well his fuse was already lit, burning with desire, and aching to be snuffed out once again. "What you have is a self-igniting fuse. You don't need any help from me."

Nash latched his arms around her body and flipped onto his back, pulling her on top of him. "Okay, I'll surrender this time. You control everything."

For a split second, the idea thrilled her. He'd already blown her mind in so many ways. His muscle tone. Strength. Endurance. As if he'd ripped her open, then hand-stitched her closed, just to shred her to pieces once again. She wanted to do the same for him.

But anxiety washed over her. The last time she was on top of anything, she fell off her bunk bed and broke her arm in two places. That hardly qualified her as an expert. What the hell did she know about pleasing a man?

Shit. Absolutely nothing.

Her decision to maintain her virginity until marriage had been a stupid one. Her mother had been a pure woman when she'd married Bailey's father at a young age, and Bailey had hoped to honor her mom's memory by doing the same. But when she crept into her early twenties and was still single, she should have given up the idea behind that logic. Because the older she got, the weirder it had become to explain.

Thankfully, Nash hadn't asked her reasoning behind it. Maybe he thought it was none of his business. Or maybe it just didn't matter to him. Either way, he hadn't pushed for the details and she wasn't about to volunteer them.

For years, she'd longed to feel the intimate connection she imagined existed between two lovers, but somehow she'd always managed to tamp down her urges and suppress her desires. Hell, she'd never even masturbated before in fear that it would only make her want to give in. But after what she'd went through last night, she couldn't hold out any longer.

Just the thought of what could have happened if Nash hadn't found her in the parking lot before Richard was enough to send shivers down her spine. And although it hadn't been the only thing that factored into her decision to sleep with him, Nash coming to her rescue had definitely been at the top of the list. After she'd realized what he'd done for her, she'd felt an intimate connection with him, one she'd never shared with anyone before. One she wanted to feel again right now.

Nash slid on a condom, shifted her hips, and eased into her. She accommodated him easier now, but his breath still hissed out, as if he lowered himself into scalding water.

"Nash, I…" Heat flooded her cheeks. "I don't know how to…"

"Just move back and forth. Or up and down. Hell, side to side. It doesn't matter. You're so fucking tight that even you just breathing is driving me mad."

She swallowed hard, knowing he was doing his damnedest to keep her from feeling silly for not knowing how to pleasure him. But that didn't mean she wouldn't try. Hoping for the best, she bit her lip and started to move. Ten minutes later, they were both stretched out on the bed wearing goofy grins. Although her performance was probably more along the lines of a rodeo clown, he made her feel like a champion bull rider.

"Down for the count?" she asked, still panting.

The corners of his mouth curved, ripening into a full-on smile. "Maybe. Why don't you turn over onto your stomach." When her mouth fell open, he laughed. "No, it's not what you think."

She sighed with relief and flipped over, propping herself with a pillow. Nash held his head up with one bent elbow beside her and fanned the fingers of his free hand flat over the smooth skin on her back. As he lightly traced the subtle contours of her spine, her overexerted body basked in the sensation. Within minutes, her mind plummeted into a deep, relaxing slumber.

It seemed like only seconds had passed when her eyes fluttered open again. She glanced at the curtains on the window and noted the blue morning light peeking in. Tangled in the sheets next to her, Nash had sprawled out and was fast asleep with his face buried into the pillow.

She was tempted to curl up to him and fight for the covers, but she wasn't sure waking him was the right thing to do. Not if she wanted her vagina to one day forgive her. Truth be told, getting shagged by a man like Nash Sutherland wasn't the worst thing that could happen to a girl...unless that girl had been a virgin.

The delicious ache between her thighs reminded her why waking him would be a very bad idea. Hell, the orgasms he'd given her alone were nearly as crippling as the numerous times he'd plundered her.

Bailey rose quietly, and padded across the room, but a twinge of guilt forced her to look back at him. She hated walking out on him like this, but just like her life, her emotions were in flux. Nash was one of the good guys, but there were things he didn't know about her, things she didn't want to explain. *Maybe it's better this way.*

Silently, she slid on her dress and made her way to the kitchen. She used his phone in the kitchen to call for a cab, giving them the address she found on a piece of mail laying on the counter. Then she found her shoes and purse and headed for the front door.

Another pang of guilt stopped her in her tracks. *Damn it.*

Could she just leave without saying goodbye? No, she couldn't do that to him, not after what they'd shared. Not after he'd taken care of her the way he had. Sure, it had meant more to her than it probably had for him. But that didn't excuse bad manners.

Stepping back inside, Bailey tiptoed down the hallway and back into the bedroom, where Nash lay in the same position he'd been in when she'd left the room. Bailey pulled her lipstick out of her purse and scrawled a quick message onto the mirror over the dresser. Four short words to express her gratitude. Not the most endearing note she'd ever written, but she was in a hurry.

If she wasn't waiting outside when the taxi pulled in, the driver might honk. More importantly, she needed to get out the door before Nash woke up and caught her doing the walk of shame. After all, one-night-stands were notorious for them.

But although she had a lot of regrets about last night, sleeping with him would never be one of them. Her shame came from something else.

She'd never told Nash her real name.

Six weeks later...

BAILEY LOOKED UP with tears in her eyes. "Are you sure?"

"Yes, I'm sure. Honey, you've had a rough few months. It's all the stress you've been under. I think it's taking a toll on you. Now go home, put your feet up, and get some rest. I'll tell the other girls you'll be back in a few days."

"But I'm scheduled to work all weekend."

"One of the others will cover your shift. Either way, we'll make do. No one wants to be served by a waitress who's gagging and running to the bathroom every five minutes."

"It's the smell of the food that's—"

"If you finish that sentence, I'll fire you," her boss threatened.

As owner of the bar and grill, Danny ran a tight ship and took as much pride in the food that left the kitchen as he did the premium spirits he stocked in the bar.

She gave him a weak smile. "You know what I mean. I'm just sick to my stomach and the smells—any of them—only make it worse."

"Then do yourself a favor and go to a doctor. But don't come back until you're over this bug. Last thing I want is for you to get the other girls sick."

Bailey finished up her tables and clocked out before noon with only forty-three dollars in tips lining her pocket. She hated leaving them in a bind during the lunch rush and could've used the extra cash, but she was in no condition to stick around. Not when she couldn't shake the nausea and had already vomited twice.

On the drive home, she considered going to the emergency room, but knew she couldn't afford the hefty bill that would surely follow. With her car breaking down every other week and the debt she already had, she didn't need more financial problems. Danny had been right about that; stress was definitely playing a role.

Not long ago, she'd walked out on a man who had promised her the stars. Then, several hours later, she'd gone to bed with one who actually showed them to her. Now she couldn't even look at a horse trailer without thinking about that night. Sad thing was, she wouldn't change a thing. Well, except for maybe the part where Casanova broke the… *Oh, shit!*

Her car swerved, but she managed to correct the wheel before she ended up in the ditch. She pulled onto the shoulder and stopped.

No, it wasn't that.

Couldn't be that.

Could it?

Just that morning, she'd awakened with cramps and figured it was time for her period to start. She even remembered the exact day it would begin, too. June nineteenth. She picked up her phone and checked the date on the screen. It was the seventeenth...of July?

Oh, fuck! No way.

Her body weakened, but she wasn't sure if it was due to the illness or the idea that she could possibly be knocked up by a virtual stranger. This was exactly why everyone referred to it as reckless abandon. Though they hadn't really been reckless. At least not intentionally. Neither of them had set out to play a penile version of Russian Roulette. It had just happened, even after they—or rather *he*—had tried to protect them from it. They'd even used condoms every time afterward just to be safe.

Shit. Shit. Shit.

Maybe she was wrong. How had she missed her period for a whole month without noticing? But with all the bullshit she'd been dealing with over the past month, she knew exactly how.

Still, to be certain, she needed to check the calendar hanging on her kitchen wall.

Right now.

For her own sanity.

I just have to rule it out, that's all.

Frantically, she drove home, and within minutes, pulled into her driveway. She darted up the stairs to her small one-bedroom apartment and straight inside to her calendar, while chanting, "Please be food poisoning! Please be food poisoning!"

She didn't bother with a dramatic pause. No sense in making it into a bigger deal by pacing endlessly while trying to build up the courage to look at it. Physically, she had most of the signs of a common illness. Weak. Upset stomach. Hot flashes. Nausea. Never mind that most of the symptoms developed while she was counting the days since her last period.

Oh, fuck me.

Bailey was late. Really late. Basically, she'd missed boarding the menstruation train for the last damn month. But that didn't mean anything, did it?

She glared at the calendar again with mixed emotions. Maybe she was an idiot and counted wrong. Or maybe she had counted right and was still an idiot. Because the last thing she needed was to get herself into a predicament with a man she'd never see again...even if a small part of her wanted to.

Tears burned her eyes, but she forced them back. To be certain, she'd have to take a pregnancy test. But the idea of going to the drugstore and making that humiliating purchase made her feel even worse than she already did. So she decided to wait it out over the weekend and see if it wasn't just a stomach bug.

Surely she would know if she were pregnant.

Feeling better already, Bailey made herself a turkey sandwich, figuring it would be something she could hold down. Not a good decision. After going another round with the toilet, she brushed her teeth and settled on the couch wearing a comfy pair of old sweats and an oversized T-shirt.

She dozed in and out while listening to the sounds of the outside world vibrating through her walls: a low-flying plane, an eighteen-wheeler with obnoxious brakes, and her elderly neighbor shooing away a dog that had apparently lifted his leg on the man's bicycle.

Then someone knocked on her door.

She ignored it at first, but the persistent person on the other side decided that polite wasn't the way to go and started banging. "Christ, give me a second," she yelled as she made her way to the door and flung it open. "Who the hell do you think you—"

He leaned comfortably against her doorway with an irritated smirk. "Nash Sutherland. But you already knew that, didn't you, *Bailey?*"

What the hell?

"Nash, I…" A second went by before she registered his words. "Wait a minute. How'd you know my real name? And my address?"

He held up a thin piece of plastic she recognized.

"You stole my credit card?"

"No, the waitress who served you at the bar saw me recently and said you forgot it when you stormed out that night. I told her I'd get it back to you."

"Oh." Bailey shrugged. "Well, I called and reported it missing over a month ago. It's no good now. But that still doesn't explain how you found me."

"Your real name's on it, and I googled you to get the rest. Bailey Hobbs, twenty-six years old, resides at 315 Morgan Street, and wants every guy who takes her virginity to call her *Sheila*. It's amazing what you can find on the internet these days."

Her cheeks heated as the memory of that night flashed through her mind. "I *was* a virgin, damn it!"

His eyes glazed over, and he blew out a hard breath. "Sweetheart, you couldn't have fooled me otherwise, even if you wanted to. But your name sure the hell isn't Sheila. You lied about that."

She put her hands on her hips. "I didn't lie! At least not to *you*. You heard me give the other guy in the bar a line about my name being Sheila."

"You didn't correct me, though."

"Because I walked out. And you never asked me my name, anyway. Guess you were too worried about getting into my pants."

Uninvited, he stepped inside and closed the door behind him. "Look who's talking. You got what you wanted and hauled ass before I woke up. No goodbye. Nothing."

"What? I said goodbye. The note on the mirror…"

"*'Thanks, I needed that!'* was not a goodbye."

"Well, excuse me for not being an expert on one-night-stands. I thought that's how it's done. A clean break. You know, no awkward morning after."

"You've seen too many damn movies," he said, huffing out another breath. "The only thing that would've been awkward the next morning were all the positions I planned to put you in."

Mentally, she gasped. *Jesus. That's like having the winning raffle ticket, but not knowing I needed to be present to win.* Her pulse quickened, but she shook the images of his naked body out of her head. Damn it. They were getting off track. "Why were you looking for me, anyway?"

His blue eyes flickered over her face, and he frowned. "You look like hell."

"Oh, to compliment me," she said, scowling. "Thanks for that. Now if you'll excuse me…" She tried to push him toward the door, but he didn't budge.

"What's wrong with you? You look…sick." His eyebrow quirked into an abnormally high position and his gaze lowered to her stomach.

Oh, great.

She knew exactly what he was thinking. "I'm sick, not pregnant."

"Well, maybe you should take a test to prove it."

His immediate distrust pissed her off. "What, you don't believe me?"

"No, *Sheila*, I don't. But who could blame me after you gave me a false name and then ran out on me?"

"You're a real jackass, you know that? You *assumed* my name was Sheila, then have the nerve to show up at my front door and accuse me of lying to you. If you do this with all the ladies you've slept with, then it's no wonder you don't get more than one night with a woman."

His sighed and grasped her arm lightly. "Come on, I'm taking you to a doctor."

"No!" she yelled, slinging his arm off hers. "Didn't you hear a word I just said? I'm *not* pregnant."

"Then you won't mind proving it."

"I don't have to prove anything to *you*. Go away and leave me alone."

He narrowed his eyes. "I never close a door without seeing what's on the other side first. So, *Bailey*, if you want me out of here, then you're going to have to prove it to me first."

She sighed with frustration.

Not only was Nash Sutherland the most demanding and infuriating man on the planet, but he had the worst timing ever. Wreckage from the last head-on collision she had with a man still littered the ground around her. There was no room in her life for another brick wall. Even if she did have his baby on board.

Just the idea of being possibly knocked up by him made her stomach hurt more. She needed time to figure this out before she brought him in on any of it. And the only way to get that time was to make him leave. Now. "Look, I already took a pregnancy test earlier today."

He rolled his eyes dismissively. "Yeah, right."

"Again you don't believe me? Wow, you're a real jackass, you know that?" She gestured nonchalantly toward the bathroom. "Go look for yourself. The test is in the box in the bathroom trashcan. Oh, by the way, it's negative, you lunatic."

She thought for sure with all of her bravado that he wouldn't actually go and look for himself. But the untrusting bastard did just that. *Shit*.

He stormed into the bathroom and seconds later marched right back out with an empty trashcan. "I may be a lunatic, sweetheart, but at least I'm not a fucking liar."

CHAPTER SIX

NASH WAS FURIOUS.

He had never spoken to a woman like that before, but he couldn't believe she had lied so easily to his face about something so important. Especially after what they'd shared. For over a month, he hadn't been able to get her out of his head. He'd wanted to see her again, touch her again. Now, it felt like she'd punched him in the gut. "Come on, I'm taking you to my family's doctor."

"No."

"Goddamnit, Bailey. Why the hell not?"

"I'm not pregnant, okay? I woke up cramping this morning, so I'm sure I'm about to start my period any time now. If it doesn't start by Monday, I'll go get checked out."

Dread filled him and his heart pounded harder. "But if you are pregnant, you could be miscarrying. That's one of the signs."

Bailey paused, as if she hadn't even thought of it as a possibility. "Okay, fine. Then I'll go to the low-cost clinic around the corner."

"You don't have to do that. I can pay—"

"No! I don't want you to pay for anything. I already told you, I'm not pregnant."

He sighed. "Fine, but I'm driving."

"No, I—"

"Damn it. Don't fight me on this, Bailey. Just get into the damn truck."

Surprising enough, she did as he asked without arguing. *Thank God.* But they sat in silence all the way over to the clinic. No doubt she was scared and probably didn't want to be alone, but Nash had his own selfish reasons for driving her. He needed to know if this woman was carrying his unborn child or not, and apparently, he couldn't trust her to be honest about it.

Not only that, but he was worried...for her. Even if she wasn't pregnant with his child, the desire to make sure *she* was okay was unnervingly strong.

After registering at the front desk as a walk-in, they waited for a half hour before her name was finally called. She didn't seem surprised when Nash stood and followed her back. A short, plump nurse wearing pink scrubs and a serious face showed them to a back room, stopping him from entering until after Bailey had changed into a gown. Once she allowed him entry, the nurse pointed to a chair in the corner and banished him to it.

The nurse checked Bailey's vitals, noting that her blood pressure was a little high. "Probably stress-related," she said, never looking up from her chart. It was as if she were speaking to herself rather than the patient.

Bailey tolerated the nurse's abruptness, but Nash couldn't help but grind his teeth across the room. He didn't like it one bit. Or the nurse. The woman had the sourness of a pickle. But what did he really expect? Bailey was an uninsured patient with an unconfirmed pregnancy who was at a low-cost clinic because she couldn't afford to pay for her care. At least that's how the nurse probably looked at it.

But Nash *could* afford it. Not only did he have his own law practice, but he was a goddamn Sutherland. His family had made billions in the oil field after his grandparents, Bud and Celia Sutherland, struck it rich during the oil rush. Once they'd turned Sutherland Industries over to their five children—one of whom was Nash's father—his grandparents retired to live out their days on White Willow Ranch just outside of Houston.

His family would be horrified if they learned he'd taken the possible mother of his child to a low-cost clinic when the Sutherlands had their own private doctors and team of specialists in nearby Houston.

"I had some minor cramping this morning. If I am pregnant, does that mean I'm losing the baby?" Bailey asked, unable to mask the worry in her tone.

Her fearful eyes met Nash's from across the room, and his heart squeezed in his chest. She was as concerned as he was. "The doctor will talk to you about that," the gruff nurse responded as a man in dark blue scrubs entered the room. "I'm Dr. Britton," he said, not bothering to offer a comforting smile. "I don't want to speculate at this point. Let me do a pelvic exam, get a blood test, and then we'll see where we stand." He pulled some purple latex gloves from a wall dispenser and snapped them on. "Why don't you tell me what's going on with you while I take a quick look?"

The doctor was all business. Nash didn't know which was worse—the nurse's salty attitude or the doctor's acidic voice. Dr. Britton instructed Bailey to lie back and place her feet in the stirrups as if she were going on a leisurely trail ride rather than waiting for news of a possible miscarriage. No feeling. No compassion. Just the doctor's shitty, unfeeling tone, which was pissing him off.

Nervously, Bailey rattled off all of her symptoms.

"You're a bit older than most girls we see for a pregnancy test," the doctor said, sounding like a callous ass. "Are you married, Ms. Hobbs?"

Bailey told him no and closed her eyes, her cheeks reddening more and more by the second. *Damn it. The fucker is embarrassing her.* Nash's need to know if she was pregnant outweighed his ability to whisk her out the door, but he'd be damned if he let anyone make her feel bad about what had transpired between them.

"Can we get on with it, Doc?" Nash said rudely.

Cold silence filled the room, but Bailey's eyes lifted and met Nash's gaze head on. Her lips turned up in a little appreciative smile.

The doc sat on a small stool and wheeled it over between Bailey's legs. The thin, yellow sheet covering her waist suddenly seemed too small. Nash never dreamed he would be watching another man touch Bailey intimately. It felt perverse. Not only that, it grated on his last fucking nerve. And she didn't seem to like the awkwardness of it any more than he did.

The nurse hovered in the background, forced to remain in the room while the doctor performed a pelvic exam on a female patient. She would probably hold that against them as well.

When the doctor finished his exam, he allowed Bailey to sit up. "Everything looks fine," he said nonchalantly. "Just to be safe, though, I'm going to run a full panel of bloodwork, along with the pregnancy test."

As the doctor wrote in Bailey's chart, the nurse used her as a pin cushion, poking her with something the size of a knitting needle. Bailey bit her lip so hard that Nash would've sworn she punctured it. He almost wished she would have since the nurse could have just collected the blood from there and saved herself the trouble of finding the elusive vein. After bandaging the hole she'd drilled into Bailey's arm, the nurse left the room, carrying two vials of blood with her.

Dr. Britton started out the door behind her, but stopped long enough to say, "Shouldn't take long. I'll be back just as soon as I get the results."

Bailey sat there with a tense posture, staring at the floor with a heavy-lidded, tearful gaze that took his breath away. She was obviously distraught and overcome with emotion. And hell, he couldn't blame her.

Nash moved to her side and rested his hip against the table. "You okay?"

She closed her eyes and only nodded, which he imagined was to keep herself from falling completely apart. Everything was cold. The room. The vinyl table. The medical staff. So he offered her the one thing he thought she needed most right now. He slid his arm around her, nestled her into his chest, then linked the fingers of his free hand with hers.

Bailey opened her eyes before she allowed her body to relax against his supportive frame. Then she sighed contentedly. The sound pleased him.

"My buddy's wife is having a baby," Nash told her, making conversation to pass the time. "She'd pee on one of those stick tests, and he'd get all tied up in knots while they waited for their results, every single time. Now I guess I know how he felt."

"Every time?"

"Yeah, they were trying to get pregnant. Took a few months before it happened, but they finally did it."

Bailey considered what he said for a moment and then looked confused. "You mean they did this to themselves... *on purpose?*"

He grinned. "Well, some people actually want children."

Her face turned three shades whiter, and she looked like she was about to pass out. Visibly shaken, she leaned further against him and clutched at her stomach, as if a sudden wave of nausea rolled through her.

"Hey, are you okay?" Nash steadied her and put the back of his hand to her forehead, checking for fever.

"I've been sick for a week. I thought I'd bounce back by now, but it's not getting any better."

"Sweetheart, if you *are* pregnant, you're probably going to feel this way for a while." He eased her forward and rubbed his hand up and down her back. "Is that better?"

"Yes, thank you."

He didn't believe her, though, because she looked even more pale and brittle than before, obviously trying to hold herself together still. Nash reasoned that her feelings were probably being batted back and forth like an emotional birdie in a really fucked up game of badminton. God knew his were. After all, she could be carrying his...

Shit. Wait. Was it even his?

Nash smoothed a hand over his face. He hadn't seen her in six weeks, and although he'd been looking for her since the day she'd snuck out on him, she obviously hadn't done the same. After all, she knew where he lived. Was it possible she'd moved on and had been with someone else since the night they'd spent together?

The thought alone sent a chill through him and knotted his stomach. Call him possessive, but he didn't like the thought of another man touching her like he had. And although he felt like a jerk, he needed to know for certain.

"Look, I know this is probably going to sound bad, but I don't want to assume anything, so I need to ask you something important," he said, preparing her for his blunt question. "If you are pregnant, is it...I mean, the baby...is it mine?"

The outrage in her eyes told him everything he needed to know. "I can't believe you asked me that." She crossed her arms and glared at him. "What kind of woman do you take me for?"

"I know you aren't—"

"Don't presume you know anything about me."

Nash placed his hand on her shoulder. "Okay, I'm sorry. I didn't meant to upset you. I just wanted to be sure."

"Well, how would you feel if someone questioned your morals? Maybe I should ask you the same question and see how you like it."

He grinned, but said nothing.

"Oh, so now you think this is funny?"

"No, but if you ask me if the baby is *yours*, I promise not to get mad."

She sighed. "Okay, so it sounded stupid. But I was making a point."

"Point taken," he said, nodding. "It's insulting. I get it. But you didn't tell me your real name. And you never mentioned you were a virgin, either."

"What does that have to do with anything? You got what you wanted."

He lifted a brow. "And you didn't?"

"You're making it sound like I asked for this, Nash. As if I wanted to wind up pregnant from one careless night with a total stranger." Her voice wavered and her fingers twisted together in her lap as she became more upset.

"Look, I already said I was sorry the condom broke."

Bailey looked like she wanted to cry, but her words came out laced with sarcasm. "Yeah, you were so sorry that you had me twice more afterward." She glanced over, just as the corner of his mouth quirked a little. "Go ahead and smile, Nash. You've proven yourself," she said in a mocking tone. "You're a Grade A stud."

His grin dissipated. "Okay, let's not bullshit each other. The situation isn't ideal. But if you are pregnant, we have a lot to work out and—"

"There's nothing to work out. I know what I would have to do."

Nash grimaced, realizing she had said *I* instead of *we*. Obviously, she wasn't planning on including him in whatever decision she made. But what could he do about it? It's not like he could make her have his baby if she didn't want to. *Christ. Was that what she was getting at?*

Panic gripped him by the throat, forcing his voice to soften. "Are you considering abortion?"

"No," she said easily.

Relief washed over him and he inhaled a deep breath. He always knew one day he would have a child, but until this very moment, he hadn't known he was ready to be a father. Yet, he somehow was. "Oh, thank God. I thought you were going to say—"

"You'll need to sign over your parental rights."

His head snapped toward her and fire flickered behind his eyes. "You're not putting *my* baby up for adoption."

"No, I…I'd keep the baby. But I'll need to save up some money until the baby is born. I'll have to move in with my father for a while and my dad lives in a remote part of Alaska. That isn't going to keep us in proximity to you. It'd be the best thing for both—"

"Hold up. Just stop right there, Bailey. Where the fuck do you get off?"

"Oh, come on. You know it would be the most sensible thing to do. It would be easier for you, me, and the baby. What else would we do—shuffle the kid back and forth between us? It would be confusing to a child."

"Forget it. It's not going to happen," he said, shaking his head. "I'd never sign away the rights to my own child. And you're not taking off to Alaska so my child can be eaten by a bear or attacked by a fucking moose. I'm a lawyer. I know all about my parental rights, and I'll get a court order to keep you here if I have to."

Her eyes widened and her mouth dropped open slightly. She was clearly stunned and didn't know what to say. Nash hadn't meant to threaten her with a court order, but he couldn't bear the thought of her leaving and taking his child away from him…even if it was only a fictional baby at the moment.

His own parents had split up when he was only two, and though he completely understood why his mom had left his dad, he couldn't bear to think his own child would grow up while living in a separate household from him. There had to be another way.

"Nash, please don't make this any more difficult than it already is. I won't be able to afford my apartment. What happened is done, and we can't undo it. You hooked up with a woman and got lucky. It doesn't have to be anything more than that for you."

Unable to contain his anger, he shot up off the table. "That's bullshit and you know it." He paced back and forth before stopping directly in front of her. "If I had that attitude, I'd be considered a douche bag, deadbeat father. But since you're the woman, you can say it and make it sound like you're doing me a favor. It's a fucking catch-22."

"I know it's an uncomfortable situation we're in, but I *am* doing you a favor. I'm absolving you of any responsibility to this child."

"I didn't ask to be absolved of anything, did I? My ingredients were used in the mix, which means this baby is half mine. If you don't want to co-parent, that's fine. Then you can pop it out and hand it over."

Bailey blinked at him. "I'm not an Easy Bake Oven, you jackass! And you're *not* taking the baby away from me after I carry it for nine months. You can forget it."

Nash shrugged. "Well, partner, then it looks like we're in this together."

CHAPTER SEVEN

BAILEY HELD HER breath and stared impatiently at the door. Several minutes had passed and Nash hadn't said a word. He only measured her with his eyes and seemed to be rolling something around in his head. That worried her even more.

She hadn't expected him to get so upset and react the way he had when she'd asked him to sign over his parental rights. Hell, she'd given him an out…and he hadn't taken it. And his refusal to do so was seriously one of the most admirable and sexiest things she'd ever seen.

No, wait. I don't want him to want the baby. It would only complicate things.

Why couldn't he be one of those guys who walked away? Lots of women got into situations where the father of the baby didn't want to be involved. Of all the guys she could've slept with, how did she end up with a *man* who wanted to act like one? *God, he'd never leave her alone now.*

The moment he'd thrown the court order in her face, she knew she was in trouble. Nash would win any custody battle she threw at him. He was a lawyer, for goodness sakes! Surely, he knew the law and any loopholes in it. He would be familiar with the judges and know exactly which ones would be most sympathetic to the father over the mother. And if that wasn't enough, he'd certainly bring their financial situations and living arrangements into play. In the end, he would walk away with sole custody.

Unless…

Maybe she could convince Nash that the baby wasn't his. When he'd asked her, she hadn't actually said the baby was his. She'd only suggested it. But if she mentioned the other man in her life, Nash would probably assume the worst. Thus far, he'd always seemed to when it came to her. Then again, knowing him, he'd probably just insist on a paternity test. She had to try, though.

Just as she opened her mouth to speak, the doctor stepped back into the room. "You're pregnant. About six weeks along, going off your last menstrual cycle."

Jeez. Thanks for blurting that out. Perfect timing, asshole.

"Okay," she said, trying to hide her irritation.

"I'm putting you on bedrest for a couple of days, which may help with the cramping. Your bloodwork came back normal, and I'm giving you a prescription for some prenatal vitamins. If your cramps worsen, you develop fever, or have any bleeding, then go to the nearest emergency room. And don't forget to follow up with your regular OB doctor as soon as possible."

"I don't have a—"

"She will," Nash said, cutting her off.

The doctor didn't bat an eye at the interruption. He just looked directly at Nash and said, "No sex or anything else in your vagina for at least forty-eight hours." Then he walked out the door.

"His bedside manner sucks," Nash said with annoyance. "He didn't even ask you if you had any questions."

"I didn't."

"Well, maybe *I* did. I get the whole no sex thing, but what the hell kind of strange shit did he think I'd be sticking in your vagina?"

Bailey bit her cheek to keep from smiling. "He meant no tampons or douching."

"Then why did he look at me when he said it? It's *your* vagina."

"Can you quit saying…that word? It sounds so vulgar coming from you."

"Hey, he called it that first," Nash said with a laugh. "If it was me, I'd call it a puss—"

She clamped her hand over his mouth just as the nurse opened the door. The woman sneered at them and shook her head like she was perturbed. "Be sure to stop and see the receptionist on your way out."

To get them the hell out of there, Bailey hurried behind the curtain and quickly changed her clothes. When she came out, Nash glanced down her body and smirked. Her gaze followed his to see what the hell he was looking at. "Did I miss something? Why are you smiling?"

"You're pregnant," he replied, the smile spreading wider. "With *my* baby."

"We already figured that, genius."

"Yeah, but now it's confirmed." He grinned again, like it was the newsflash of the century. "You can't try to get rid of me now by saying the baby isn't mine. That *is* what you were planning, right?" Sure of himself, he cocked an eyebrow at her. "It won't work. The doc pegged it down to almost the precise day we were together."

Damn him and his perceptiveness. She hated that the gears turning in her head showed so plainly on her face. It made her want to wipe that stupid grin off his face, so she shrugged nonchalantly. "That's right...*if* you were the only man I'd had sex with around that time."

His smile melted. "You lied about that, too?"

The worried look of desperation in his eyes made her feel like a jerk. She wanted to lie, but couldn't bring herself to do it. Not to him. Not about the baby. She sighed heavily. "No, Nash, I wasn't with anyone else. Just you."

The look of relief on his face only made her feel guiltier. Damn it.

They headed down the hallway toward the checkout counter and waited for an old woman behind the desk to pull up Bailey's file on her computer. "How much can you afford to pay today?"

Bailey practically cringed as she pulled out her checkbook.

"All of it," Nash said, quickly fishing his wallet from his back pocket and sliding the receptionist a credit card.

"Um, sir. Since Ms. Hobbs doesn't have medical coverage and her income is low enough, we won't charge her for the full amount."

"Ms. Hobbs isn't responsible for the bill. *I* am. Just tell me what I owe and I'll pay for it in full."

"Well, the entire bill is over three hundred dollars."

Nash gave the old woman a quick nod. "That's fine."

She smiled and took his card without so much as glancing at Bailey, who stood there with her mouth open and arms crossed.

Nash signed the receipt and then steered her toward the parking lot before she could argue with him.

This was exactly what she didn't want. She didn't want to be a financial burden on a complete stranger…or to put her trust in another man. As she waited for Nash to unlock the passenger door, she said, "I'll pay you back."

"Like hell you will." He opened the door and lifted her into the seat. "That's *my* baby you're carrying. I'm capable of paying for the care you and our child receive."

She shook her head so hard she made herself dizzy. "Nash, I can't accept—"

"Look, if you want to argue about this, we will. But I'm warning you…you'll lose. I'm a lawyer. I do this shit for a living." Without another word, he closed the door on her protests and strolled around to the driver's side.

They headed for Bailey's apartment. Nash was exceptionally quiet, and although she could tell he was carefully mulling something over in his head, he said nothing. Once inside, Bailey sat down on the couch, hoping they could talk and she could try to reason with him once more.

Granted, he was a lawyer who probably made a lot more money than she did and could financially support a child. But that's also exactly what scared her. Nash was used to getting his way. If co-parenting didn't work out, would he try to gain sole custody of the baby because he had the better means to care for a child? And if so, would she ever see her son or daughter again?

Having grown up without her mother in her own life, Bailey couldn't risk it. She hated to think Nash would be so cruel, but if her past had showed her anything, it was that she wasn't a good judge of character when it came to men. "Nash, what I said earlier about you giving up your rights… Please think about it. You can't possibly want to be a part-time father to this child. It'd never work."

Nash knelt down in front of her. His eyes trained on her stomach, then his warm hand quickly followed. Bailey tensed and put her hand on top of his as his gaze flickered back to hers. "Marry me, then."

She jerked her hand back, as if his words had somehow scalded her. "W-what did you say?"

"You heard me. I want you to marry me."

To him, he probably thought he was stepping up, acting like a man, and taking responsibility for his actions. But to her, it was more like a rude awakening littered with strange emotions that no doubt flickered across her face one by one. Shock. Fear. Intrigue. Distrust.

"Listen, I'm not going to water it down for you. It's a crapshoot, I know. But I want to help you—"

"No."

"Just think about it for a while. You don't have to answer right now."

"I gave you an answer. I said no."

"Damn it, Bailey. Why not?"

She shook her head, not believing he even needed to ask. "Are you kidding me? Nash, you're a nice guy, and I always thought the man who took my virginity would be the man I grew old with, but this situation isn't anything like I'd pictured."

"So plans change."

"But people don't. I can't marry you for security. That isn't what a marriage should be based on. I believe in the sanctity of marriage. What I don't believe in is marrying a complete stranger on a whim because we couldn't keep our hormones in check."

"Then we're perfect for each other. I don't believe in divorce. Never have. I've always planned to have a family one day. Might as well be now. We'll make it work."

"We hardly even know each other."

"Living together will make it easier for that to happen, though."

"It won't work, Nash. Trust me, you wouldn't like living with me. I get moody sometimes."

"You're already moody. I'm not worried about that."

She let out a heavy breath. "I'm being serious. It would be a marriage based on a lie...on a pregnancy. I'm sorry, but I don't want a husband just on paper."

"Good, because that wasn't what I was suggesting. It would be a real marriage, Bailey. I'd be the loyal, doting husband and father, while you would be my lovely wife and mother of our child. We'd share the same bed and everything. I wouldn't ask you to give anything up." He gave her a smug grin and shrugged his eyebrows at her. "Especially when it comes to sex."

She pushed him out of her way and stood up alarmingly fast. Then she walked over and opened the front door. "Get out," she said, narrowing her eyes.

"What's wrong?"

"You mean besides that insulting, detached proposal you offered me?"

Nash stood up and walked closer, but didn't dare try to touch her. That was probably a smart move because she was seething mad. But he apparently wasn't about to let her throw him out without giving it another shot. "Bailey, I want this to work."

"No, what you want is for us to be paper dolls living together in a stiff cardboard-constructed home with no passion or feelings. You want polite, fake smiles during breakfast and meaningless pity fucks after dinner. Well, no thank you."

"Sweetheart, you misunderstood. My parents' marriage was much like that. That's not what I want for us. If you'll just let me—"

"There's no *us*," she said firmly. "I can't marry you, anyway."

"You mean you *won't* marry me."

She hesitated, then dropped her gaze. "Both," she said. "Now I want you to go."

He eyed her suspiciously. "Wait. You're not telling me something. What is it?"

"I asked you to leave."

Nash shut the door and turned to face her. "What is it you're not saying?"

"Stop it. I…I don't want to lie to you anymore."

"Then don't." He cocked his head to the side, waiting for an answer. "Come on, Bailey. Tell me why you *can't* marry me."

Tears welled up in her eyes. "Because…I'm already married."

The look on his face crushed her.

It had been an undeniable mix of confusion and frustration. Nash couldn't understand how she had been married—virginity intact—to one man, now impregnated by another, yet still completely alone. Sad thing was, she didn't understand it herself. But she'd already married one man for the wrong reasons. She wasn't about to repeat the mistake.

"So you're saying that this baby could possibly be...your husband's?"

"No, it's not his."

"You were with someone else, then?" He rubbed at his temples. "Jesus. How many men have there been?"

God, all of this is going wrong. "Nash, I...no, you're the only man I've ever been with."

His eyes blazed fire. "Don't screw with me, Bailey. You said you're married, for Christ's sake. Don't you dare tell me you haven't slept with your—"

"It's true!" she cried, embarrassment slapping her face and stinging both cheeks.

He snorted and rolled his eyes. "Okay, fine. I'll play your stupid game. Then what the hell were you doing on your wedding night?"

She blinked rapidly, forcing back the building tears. "You."

CHAPTER EIGHT

NASH WASN'T SURE what to believe.

When she'd turned down his marriage proposal, Nash understood her need to choose a life partner based on love, rather than necessity. Hell, he felt the same way. But arranged marriages had been around for centuries and many were successful once the couple grew to love each other. In time, he thought they would do the same. After all, she was the mother of his unborn child. That alone made him care more for her than just some one-night stand. Not that she'd ever been that to him, anyway.

From the moment the waitress had given him Bailey's credit card, Nash had hoped he would find her and it would be the start of something between them. Sure, he'd been pissed to find out she'd never told him her real name. And yes, it had annoyed him that she'd never bothered to show up on *his* doorstep, though she knew where he lived. Now it all made sense.

But she's married? Fuck.

What the hell was he supposed to do about that? And where the hell was her husband, anyway? If Bailey was thinking about moving in with her father, then that meant her spouse wasn't in the picture—at least not fully. Was he alive? Was he out of town?

So many questions ran through his mind, but he couldn't ask her a single one. The bomb she'd dropped on Nash had stunned him into silence, and before the shock wore off enough for him to speak, Bailey had run into her bedroom, slamming the door behind her. Clearly, she wanted to be alone, which was fine by him, since he needed time to think as well.

Either way, he was involved now, which seemed to be the very thing she didn't want. *Well, tough shit.* The idea of her taking off with his baby to parts unknown was ludicrous, especially when he had the means to take care of both of them. Like it or not—husband or not—Nash wasn't going anywhere. And although she didn't know it yet, neither was she. And he'd make damn sure of it.

After a half hour passed, he tapped on the bedroom door and pushed it open. Bailey lay on the bed and tilted her head up until her glossy eyes met his. "Nash? W-what are you doing back here?" She sniffled.

"I never left. Are you all right?"

She tensed and her lips flattened into a thin, grim line. "I-I'm fine."

"You're not fine. But it's okay. We don't have to figure anything out tonight. I can plainly see the thought alone stresses you out, which is the last thing you need right now. I don't want to do anything to put our child in danger."

Our child. He liked the sound of that.

Her body relaxed a little. "I just want to change and go to bed." She got up and walked over to her dresser and pulled out some clothes, then headed into the bathroom.

He pulled the comforter back and arranged the pillows while waiting for her to come back out. When she did, he gave her a stern look.

"What?" she asked casually, as if she wasn't standing there in a tiny pair of shorts and a tight tank top with no bra that showed her hard nipples.

He nodded to her attire. "Could've warned me."

"I normally sleep in much less, but I couldn't very well walk out here half-naked, now could I?"

He groaned under his breath and resisted the urge to shift the instant swelling in his groin area. God, he wanted to touch her, but he couldn't… *Damn woman's trying to kill me.*

Despite her insistence that she could do it herself, Nash helped her into the bed and quickly covered her with the sheet. It was either that or risk doing something that was surely against doctor's orders. But he wasn't planning on leaving her all by herself, so he sat on the edge of the bed and kicked off his boots.

"What are you doing?"

"Getting comfortable. I don't plan on sleeping with these on my feet." He pulled at his plaid shirt, unsnapping all the buttons simultaneously before sliding it off his shoulders and down his arms.

Her eyes widened as she sat up. "You can't stay here!"

"Why? Is your husband coming home?" He smiled when she didn't answer him. "I didn't think so." *Hoped was more like it.*

"It's just that…well, I…" She drew in a deep breath, willing herself to speak, but nothing came out.

"Like I said, we don't have to talk about it right now. I'd like an explanation, but it can wait until you're feeling better. Get some rest."

She let out a sigh, which sounded very much like relief, and did as he asked. He walked around to the other side of the bed, slid in next to her, then pulled the covers over both of them.

"What are you doing now?" she asked, throwing the covers off once again.

"Going to sleep."

"Not here, you're not."

"Your couch is two feet shorter than I am. So, yes, *here.* Besides, this is not the first time we've been in a bed together." And if he had it his way, it wouldn't be the last.

"Just had to bring that up, didn't you?" She didn't miss the grin he wore. "Fine. But stay on your own side." Bailey flipped over, facing away from him as he hiked the blanket up higher on her thigh.

He chuckled at the irritation in her voice and turned off the lamp next to the bed, plunging them into darkness. "No problem."

Within minutes, her breathing evened out and she fell asleep. Guess fatigue won out over frazzled nerves and rushing hormones. Of course, that didn't solve the problem he was having with *his* rushing hormones. At least until she started snoring. It was the single most unsexy sound he'd ever heard.

As she breathed in, a winch tightened in her nasal passages, then the air vibrated past her lips with a gurgling flair. It was quite remarkable such a tiny woman could make such a big noise. He smiled, though. The mother of his unborn child was the bedtime version of Darth Vader.

And, one way or another, she was going to be his wife.

CHAPTER NINE

EARLY THE NEXT morning, Bailey awoke in the cold sweat of a full-blown panic attack. Fear consumed her, and she mentally gasped as her eyes shot open. In her dream, not only had her body threatened miscarriage, but she'd lost the baby and the nurse was holding her down while the doctor performed a D&C procedure.

She was on her back, staring at the ceiling of her dimly lit bedroom. Nash's protective hand lay gently over her stomach, covering the baby growing inside her womb. *His baby.* She swallowed hard, but didn't move.

From an early age, all she'd ever wanted was to be with a kind, decent man while carrying his child. Only she'd pictured a married couple deeply in love waiting patiently for the birth of their child. Not a man and a woman who barely knew each other, with their lives suddenly threaded together by an unplanned pregnancy.

Nash's hand twitched on her stomach, then slid under the edge of her shirt. His warm fingers whispered across her skin and settled just above the waistband of her low-cut shorts, as if he was subconsciously trying to get closer with a more intimate touch.

She mentally sighed at the mess she'd gotten herself into.

Why couldn't he just walk away and leave her to deal with this on her own? Hell, he hadn't even pushed her to tell him the truth about her husband because he hadn't wanted to stress her out. As if he were already putting her and the baby's needs above his own. Damn. Why did Nash have to be so...kind and decent?

Sure, he probably thought asking her to marry him was the noble thing to do. But Nash didn't love her any more than she loved him. And, like it or not, he obviously thought of her and the baby as a package deal, a duet of sorts, which was something he'd made immediately clear with his crazy marriage proposal.

She shouldn't even be considering it, and the fact that she was terrified the hell out of her. Because the last thing she wanted was for him to feel trapped and end up resenting her for it. And that's exactly what would happen if she married him.

He was the kind of guy any woman could easily fall for, but that was part of the problem. She didn't want to fall for him. Not when it would only end in heartbreak later. Hers, not his. So why set herself up for it? After all, she'd already learned the hard way that men fell into bed, not in love.

Why did things have to happen this way? If only she had recognized the symptoms earlier in the week, then she could've kept him from finding out about the baby and she could've left free and clear. No one would've ever had to know who the father of her baby was. It's not like anyone else would have asked about... Damn.

The baby.

The child would eventually want to know. Even if she could get Nash to surrender his rights—which would happen when hell started passing out deep freezers—eventually their child would grow up and ask the question, "Where's my daddy?" Then what would she do?

The thought made her queasy and she groaned. She eased out of the bed and went into the bathroom, hovering over the toilet while feeling weak and faint. She salivated and gagged constantly, but nothing came up. After brushing her teeth, she opened the bathroom door to find Nash sitting on the edge of the bed waiting for her with a worried look on his face.

He measured her with his eyes. "You okay?"

"Just a little nauseated."

"Any cramping?"

"No. I think I just overdid it at work yesterday morning. Getting off my feet helped a lot."

He stood and stretched his arms, then ran his fingers through his unruly hair. "Are you hungry? I could make you something to eat."

"I always eat breakfast at work, so you probably won't find much in the kitchen beyond some stale corn flakes and soured milk. Oh...God." She groaned and clutched her mouth, suddenly feeling sick again.

As she sat shakily on the bed, he grabbed a nearby trashcan and placed it beside her. "Well, you have to eat something. I'm going to call my office and let my secretary know that I'm not coming in today, and then I'll run to the nearest grocery store. I'll fill your prescription for the prenatal vitamins while I'm out, but I want you to stay in bed until I get back."

She uncovered her mouth. "Wait. What am I supposed to do all day?"

"Avoid stress." Nash turned on the TV across the room and tossed her the remote. "Here, catch up on your soap operas."

"I don't watch soap operas."

"You do now." He chuckled and started toward the bedroom door, but stopped before going through it. "If you can think of anything you might need for me to pick up before I leave, just holler. I'm leaving in ten minutes." Then he stepped out, shutting the door behind him.

She glared at the door. "I can feel my stress reducing already," she called out, not sure if he'd even heard her.

TWO DAYS OF constant bed rest was enough to make anyone grouchy, especially Bailey. Oh, sure, she had been allowed to get up—once every hour for her bathroom break, where she lingered over the toilet willing herself to puke. Nothing ever came out, though.

If she could only throw up just once while in the bathroom, she'd be happy. She hated the idea of upchucking in front of him and had refused to use the trashcan he gave her. There was nothing attractive about a girl gagging and dry-heaving. Ever.

It was irritating enough that every time she came out of the bathroom, Nash was waiting outside the door, ready to steer her back to bed. Like she was in maximum security prison and he was her personal guard, assigned to torment and annoy her with his constant orders. She tolerated it because his concern for the baby outweighed any amount of bedridden testiness she felt…even if she did feel like shanking him on occasion.

She'd used her cell phone only once to let her boss know she was on doctor-ordered bed rest, but Nash made her promise to turn it off afterward. He claimed it would stress her out more, but he was wrong. The only thing stressing her right now was him pretending to be her warden. But time had been served by this prisoner, and today she was a free woman. *Halleluah!*

No more reruns of *Roseanne*. No more melodramatic soap operas. And no more lying in that stupid-ass bed that she'd begun to loathe with a passion. She took her prenatal vitamin, cupping water under the bathroom faucet to wash it down with. Then she hurried to get dressed, knowing the world hadn't paused for two days, even if she had. She had something important to do and it couldn't be put off a second longer.

As she pulled on her second shoe, Nash opened the bedroom door wearing a dorky Garfield apron she'd received as a gag gift from one of her coworkers. He carried in a plate of pancakes and a glass of orange juice. He frowned as he watched her tie her shoelace. "Going somewhere?"

"I have some things to take care of."

He sat down next to her on the bed and offered her the plate. When she shook her head and waved him off, he pushed it toward her again. "Eat something. You haven't had anything yet."

"I'm not hungry."

"Well, the baby is," he said firmly. "Besides, we still need to talk."

Crap. She took the plate and started eating, hoping that with her mouth full, he wouldn't expect her to say much. She knew this was coming and was dreading every minute of it.

"We need to make some changes," he said, then paused to judge her reaction. She smiled timidly around the big bite of pancake she had just stuffed into her mouth, so he continued. "I want you to get the care you need and deserve. I called my medical insurance company this morning and found out you'll be fully covered. We won't have to pay for anything."

She swallowed. "Your insurance will cover me as the mother of your unborn child? That's odd. I didn't know they did that sort of—"

"As my wife," he corrected.

She closed her eyes and breathed out a sigh. "Nash, don't."

"Why not? You and the baby need medical coverage, and I want a relationship with my child. It's the perfect solution. I have a big house in a nice area for raising a child. I'm a responsible, honest man with a good paying job and can provide for both of you. You won't have to work during the pregnancy…or even afterward, if you don't want to. You can be a stay-at-home mom, if that's what you choose. Everything between us will be fifty-fifty."

"God, you just don't get it. There's nothing between us, Nash."

"The baby disagrees."

"Stop doing that! Quit speaking for our child and guilt-tripping me into doing things *your* way. It isn't fair to me. You don't know what this baby wants or needs any more than I do."

"I know he needs both of his parents."

"He? What do you mean *he*? Maybe it's a she. Now you're acting like you know the sex of the baby? Jesus. For someone who isn't carrying the kid, you sure know an awful lot about him." *Damn it, now he has me doing it.* "Or her," she quickly added.

He grinned lightly. "It could work, you know."

It would be so easy to declare Nash her hero and ride off into the sunset with him. But that wasn't reality, and she knew it. Her life was a hot mess right now. The last thing she needed was to complicate it further and have even more regrets when there were alternative choices to consider. She had things to do. Like call her dad, the only man she had ever truly been able to rely on.

"It won't work. And I don't want to be stuck with someone because my egg and your sperm decided to dance together. You shouldn't want that, either."

"I'm willing to give it a shot."

She set the plate down on the nightstand and rose. "Well, I'm not. Besides, I told you…I'm already married," she reminded him as she quickly made her way to the door.

"Do you love him?"

She stopped in her tracks and turned back to him slowly. "That's none of your business."

"Can you answer the question?"

She swallowed the knot that suddenly formed in her throat. "Y-yes."

"Yes, you love him? Or, yes, you can answer the question?"

Don't drag this out. Just end it now before things get worse. "Both."

Nash gave her a long, searing look, one of confusion and frustration and...pain? Yes, definitely pain. She hadn't known she could hurt him and wasn't sure why he would be upset over a stranger refusing to marry him. And why did her own chest suddenly feel heavier and her throat raw? *Damn it.*

"Look, Nash, I don't know what you want me to say. It's complicated, okay? In time, we'll figure out all the details. But, right now, I have to go. I can't be late. Just leave me your phone number on the notepad, and I'll call you when things settle down." Then she walked out of the bedroom.

As she grabbed her car keys from the key hanger and opened the front door, Nash stomped out of the bedroom at a furious pace. She ignored him and headed for her ugly brown car, but he followed right behind her.

"You have some fucking nerve, you know that?" he yelled as she unlocked her car. "You'll call me when things calm down? Yeah, right. When the hell will that be...when the kid's leaving for college?"

All around them, nosy neighbors peeked out their windows to see what the commotion was all about. "Quiet down. My neighbors can hear you."

"I don't give a damn what they hear." His eyes blazed like an inferno as he worked himself up more. "What are you afraid of? That word will get back to your husband that you not only cheated on him, but you're carrying another man's child?"

"That's it! I think it's time for you to go," Bailey sneered, wrenching open the door on her car. "In fact, don't bother coming back."

"Damn it," Nash muttered before blowing out a hard breath. "Look, I'm sorry. But we need to figure this out now."

"No, *we* don't," she said, still upset. Maybe his sky-high temper had landed safely on the ground, but hers was still soaring in the turbulent air his arrogance had left behind. "I want you to leave."

"Can't we just talk about it?"

"Because it worked out so well this time?" She checked her watch and then shook her head. "No. I don't have time for any of this. Just go."

"Fine," he huffed out. "But don't be surprised if we run into each other again...soon."

She didn't think he meant it as a threat, but it sure came across like one, which only made her eyes narrow more. "Chances are, the next time I run into you, it's going to be while I'm in my car with my foot on the gas," she said, before sliding into her vehicle and driving away.

As she headed across town, tears blurred her vision before trickling down her cheeks. There were so many loose ends to tie up before she left town, and Nash was now one of them. Her life was complicated enough without adding another person to the mix. It wasn't like she wanted to go through this alone. But she hated the idea of clinging to a man like some brittle...girl.

She was stronger than that, damn it.

But his constant reminders of what her first marriage should've been like were wreaking havoc on her brain and damaging her heart. Through his words alone, she saw a glimpse of what marriage to him could be like. Fully covered medical insurance, a nice home, a safe area to raise their baby, and a sexy husband who would love their child unconditionally and protect him—or her—with all the strength he possessed. But every time Nash pushed his marriage proposal on her, she knew what he was really thinking.

And it was the same thing she'd already thought.

She did well enough to take care of herself. How the hell was she going to take care of a baby, too?

But what he didn't know was that the moment she'd realized she was pregnant and wasn't having a miscarriage, the relief and happiness had unexpectedly overwhelmed her. Sometimes a person doesn't know how much they want something until it's almost lost.

The baby was her *something*.

CHAPTER TEN

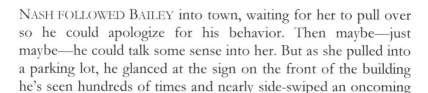

NASH FOLLOWED BAILEY into town, waiting for her to pull over so he could apologize for his behavior. Then maybe—just maybe—he could talk some sense into her. But as she pulled into a parking lot, he glanced at the sign on the front of the building he's seen hundreds of times and nearly side-swiped an oncoming car.

What the hell?

Nash drove past and parked in an adjacent lot, hiding his truck behind a row of flowering oleanders. He knew she hadn't spotted him, otherwise she'd have marched over and told him to buzz off. Instead, she climbed out of her hunk of junk and headed for the entrance to the office building.

He suspected something was going on, but wasn't sure exactly what. Maybe she was a professional con artist trying to rake him over the coals. No, that didn't make any sense. He'd offered her everything he had on a silver platter, and she hadn't accepted any of it. Medical insurance. Money. Hell, even his house. Bailey didn't seem to want anything from him. Except for him to give up his rights to...*the baby!*

Nash shook his head. Had he been that fucking gullible?

Sonofabitch. Apparently, he had.

Any time he was around Bailey, he couldn't see straight, much less use the proper head for thinking. But why was he surprised? After all, the woman had lied about her own name. Okay, so maybe she hadn't lied to *him* directly. But she'd lied to the other guy in the bar without blinking an eye. And she never bothered mentioning her real name to Nash after sleeping with him. She'd spent the entire night in his arms and hadn't bothered to say a word. But he still had no clue how deceitful she could be…until now.

His hands clenched the steering wheel as he watched her cross the parking lot and enter the lawyer's office. Nash read the sign again, hoping he'd read it wrong the first time, though he knew he hadn't. *Douglas J. Smith. Attorney specializing in Family Law.* Nope. It wasn't a mistake. Bailey was in there right now talking to a lawyer to have his parental rights stripped from him. *Damn her!*

Anger gripped his insides like an iron fist, twisting his stomach in knots. Here he was trusting she'd come around and they'd eventually get the details figured out together. Meanwhile, she plotted behind his back to take his child away. Although he knew it wouldn't be an easy task to do, especially without allegations of abuse, he wasn't about to put anything past her sneaky ass.

No wonder she kept putting him off, biding her time. Probably had planned this maneuver all along. Well, Nash wouldn't allow her to get away with it. As the baby's biological father, he had rights. And as a lawyer, he knew exactly what those rights were. If she wanted a custody battle, then he would damn sure give her one.

But just as he stepped out of the truck, Bailey walked out of the lawyer's office, escorted by a gentlemen wearing a blue suit and lugging a black briefcase. Her lawyer, Nash presumed. Then he watched them make their way across the street and disappear inside the Flat Rock courthouse.

Fuck. Bailey obviously hadn't wasted any time. Pregnant for all of two minutes and she was already filing a petition against him. And on what grounds? He'd done nothing but try to help her in any way he could.

Nash gritted his teeth together and quietly seethed as he set out for the courthouse entrance. He'd been inside the old building so many times that he barely noticed the ugly fake plants, the ancient metal detector, or the faded typed-up signs taped to the outside of the receptionist's office.

"Hey, Jill. Can I ask you something?"

The receptionist gave him a flirtatious smile, as she always did. "Sure, Nash. What can I help you with?"

"Do you know a lawyer by the name of Douglas Smith? He practices family law."

"Of course. Doug just came in with one of his clients."

Nash clenched his fist. "Which way did they go?"

"They were scheduled to appear in Judge Barclay's courtroom fifteen minutes ago, but they were running late." Jill checked the appointment book on her desk. "They'll probably have to wait until the other two cases are heard before they can go in front of the judge."

Nash blinked in astonishment. Bailey already had a court date? How the hell did she get one so fast? It was only days ago she found out she was pregnant. Even as a fucking lawyer, he couldn't have made that happen in mere days. *Fuck. Who is this woman?*

He had to give it to her, though. It was a smart move, catching him unaware and not allowing him time to build his own case. Unfortunately for her, she'd made one fatal flaw: he was aware of her bullshit plan. And the hell if he'd sit by and let her execute it.

"Is there a problem?" the receptionist asked, reading the distress on Nash's face.

"No, no problem, Jill. I just wanted to stop in and introduce myself." *As the baby's biological father.* "Can I just go up and sit in the back of the room while I wait for them to finish up?"

"I don't see why not. It's an open courtroom."

He smiled and winked at her. "Just checking. You know how these judges get a little testy if you break the rules."

She giggled. "Don't I know it."

Nash high-tailed it to the elevator, hoping he would make it to the courtroom before Bailey had a chance to talk to the judge. It wasn't the first time she had screwed him, though he doubted this encounter would be nearly as pleasurable as the last.

As he stepped into the empty elevator, the memory of that first night with her hit him with such force that he steadied himself against the cold, metal wall before hitting the button for the third floor.

That night, he'd taken her virginity—it was the only damn thing about her that he knew for sure. The moment he'd shoved into her, she couldn't have convinced him otherwise. She was so fucking tight, her inner muscles clamping onto him in a way that was most likely painful to her, but nearly caused him to lose control on the spot. *Like a damn teenager getting his rocks off for the first time.*

Even after that, he couldn't get enough of her. He spent the entire night feeding this uncanny craving he had for her responsive body, touching her intimately, thoroughly, and watching the confused yet delighted faces she pulled. She had never been touched that way—in any way—before. He knew that for sure by the way her body betrayed her, stiffening and then relaxing, with each new sensation.

His eyes closed as the memory of that night drifted over him, and a heaviness crept into his groin with an aching throb. The moment the elevator dinged its arrival on the third floor, his eyes flared open. *What the hell is wrong with me? The woman is trying to take off with my kid to some remote corner of the world, and I'm sitting here fantasizing about the little liar. I'm a goddamn fool.*

Disgusted, Nash hauled himself out of the elevator and strode down the hallway to Judge Barclay's courtroom. He slipped inside, grabbed a seat in the back, and spotted Bailey almost immediately. She sat quietly with her lawyer in the second row on the opposite side of the room, waiting for their moment with the judge.

She looked nervous, squirming in her seat and touching her fingers to her lips, but Nash didn't think she'd spied him. If anything, her lawyer had probably warned her about Judge Barclay. Everyone knew he was a hard-ass. Not only was he close to retiring, which lately had made him even surlier than normal, but the old coot was set in his ways. And Barclay liked things *his* way.

Nash hadn't realized he'd come in while the second case was wrapping up until the judge called for Bailey Hobbs to approach the bench. Shit. He had no time to prepare and wasn't sure what to do. But he had to do something.

Well, here goes…something.

"Excuse me for interrupting, Your Honor." Nash stood up and everyone, including Bailey, turned to stare at him. Her eyes widened and blinked rapidly, as if she couldn't believe he was there. "I need a word with Ms. Hobbs before this goes any further."

Judge Barclay let out a heavy breath, filled with loathing irritation. "If you need to direct your client, then you should've done so before making an appointment with my court."

Nash wasn't surprised the judge recognized him. He'd been in Barclay's courtroom twice in the last month alone. "Your Honor, Ms. Hobbs isn't my client."

That made Barclay sit up and pay attention. "Then what's the meaning of this, counselor?"

"Sir, may I approach the bench?"

"Well, I sure as hell don't mean for you to yell at me across the room," the judge said, eyeballing Nash as he made his way up the aisle and stopped next to Bailey. "This better be good, Sutherland."

Bailey looked frightened, her eyes flashing back and forth between the judge and Nash. "W-what are you doing?" she whispered.

"What I have to." He turned to face the glaring judge. "I came to stop Ms. Hobbs from trying to revoke my rights." Her head snapped up to look at him, but he continued. "She's carrying my—"

"Nash, wait!"

"No, *you* wait. Damn it, Bailey, that's my baby!"

She gasped and looked back at her lawyer, who glared angrily at her, as a low hum of voices settled over the courtroom. The judge beat his gavel on the desk several times, drawing everyone's attention.

"Order! I want order in this court!" Judge Barclay set down his gavel and squinted at them as the room became silent. "I was under the impression that this young woman was here for a dissolution of marriage. What's this about a baby, counselor?"

"The baby that Bailey…er, Ms. Hobbs, is carrying." Everyone's mouth, including Bailey's lawyer dropped open. Then Nash realized what the judge had said. "Wait…dissolution of marriage?" *Christ. She isn't here about parental rights. She's divorcing her fucking husband.*

"That's right," Bailey said, crossing her arms. "Not everything is about you, Nash."

Damn. He ran a hand over his face. She'd been so close-mouthed about her spouse that Nash hadn't considered divorce as a remote possibility. She'd said she loved her husband. Had that been a lie, too?

Bailey's lawyer turned to her with an open mouthed, wide-eyed glare. "You're pregnant?"

"Doug, I was going to tell you after—"

"You lying bitch!"

Without thinking, Nash lunged at her lawyer, grabbed him by the collar of his crisp, pressed shirt, and hauled him up on his tiptoes. "What'd you say to her, jackass?"

Bailey gasped, everyone in the courtroom jumped out of their seats, and the bailiff rushed forward to intervene. Judge Barclay put up his hand to stop him. The bailiff looked almost as surprised as Doug did.

The lawyer tried to free himself from Nash's grip. "Let go, you lunatic, or I…I'll sue your ass."

Nash got even more in his face. "I'd love to see you try, dipshit."

Bailey pulled on his bicep, though it had no effect. "Nash, stop. It's okay."

"No, it's not. He has no business talking to you like that. Not only because you're a woman, but he should never talk to a client that way."

Bailey looked again toward the judge, then back to Nash, her eyes glistening with tears. "Please, stop."

It angered him that she was protecting her dickhead lawyer, but he didn't want to cause her any more stress than she was already under. He took a slow, calming breath, and although he didn't want to, he let go of the man.

The lawyer stepped back, smoothed out the wrinkles in his shirt, and straightened his tie and jacket. "She's not my client, you moron. Bailey's my wife."

Nash stared at both of them, blinking, not sure what to say. It was a punch in the gut to hear another man say those words. But why? He knew there was a man out there tied by marriage to the mother of his child.

Then it hit him. Nash was not only jealous, but feeling territorial. He'd always hated the idea of another man laying claim to something he wanted. With Bailey, it was no different. No matter how many times he tried to reason with himself and talk himself out of it, *he* wanted her…in his bed and out.

Judge Barclay leaned back in his chair and ran his hand through his full head of gray hair. "So, let me get this straight, Ms. Hobbs. You're married to this yahoo over here," he said, pointing his gavel at Doug until Bailey nodded silently. "But you're pregnant with Bozo's baby," he said, swinging the gavel in Nash's direction. Again, she nodded. "So you're admitting that you committed adultery?"

"No, I…well, I guess, but I don't consider Doug my husband." Bailey's cheeks reddened and she lowered her head. "The day of our wedding, I caught him…with another woman."

Doug stepped forward defensively. "She doesn't have any proof. It's just her word against—"

"Oh, shut up, Doug!" Bailey lifted her head and her nostrils flared with anger. "There were over fifty guests at our wedding reception who saw me slap you and walk out while you were still trying to pull up your pants."

Nash blinked. So *that's* why she was a married virgin.

A bead of sweat broke out on Doug's forehead and he flapped his arms. "If you keep spouting this nonsense, I'll sue you for slander. I've got a reputation to uphold and—"

"Save it," Judge Barclay told him. "Tammy with the county clerk's office already let it slip that you two have been porking each other for months. When it comes to gossip, this damn courthouse is worse than a women's bathroom."

"But, Your Honor—"

"Counselor, I'm warning you. Sit down somewhere and shut up unless you want to find yourself held in contempt." Doug found the nearest seat and sank into it. Nash would've smiled if Judge Barclay hadn't given him the evil eye. "So, Mr. Sutherland," the judge asked. "Where exactly do you fit into this picture?"

Nash cleared his throat. "I met Ms. Hobbs on the night in question. She entered the venue at around—"

"Son, I don't need to hear a long-winded opening statement. Just spit it out already."

"I picked her up in a bar on her wedding night and then drove her back to my place where we…uh…"

"Consummated the marriage?" the judge asked, finishing Nash's sentence with a grin on his face. "And that was the start of your relationship, I take it?"

"Yes," Nash said, catching a glimpse of Doug shaking his head and eyeing Bailey with disgust. That guy was really asking for it. "Except that was the *only* relationship we've had for the past six weeks. It was just days ago when I found out her real name and made contact with her once again. That's when I...er, *we* realized she was pregnant."

The judge blew out a disapproving breath. "Ms. Hobbs, would you care to explain all of this nonsense?"

Bailey hesitated, but then spoke softly. "Yes."

She prattled out the details, blushing and stuttering her way through all of it. Every pair of eyes in the room was on her, all of them hanging on her every word, wanting to hear the juicy details about their relationship.

When she reached the part where Nash offered to marry her, the women in the room sighed. Even the bailiff gave him a nod of approval for being a stand-up guy. But Nash didn't care about any of that.

He only wanted to save Bailey from the embarrassment of prying eyes and tuned-up ears, yet there was nothing he could do. The judge wanted a clear-cut picture of the events as they unfolded, no matter how private they were. Even when she purposely left something out, the judge asked questions until he got at the truth. Now Judge Barclay knew everything about their situation. And so did everyone else in the room, including Bailey's dumbfuck husband.

"Okay, Mr. Smith," the judge said. "Do you have medical insurance that would cover your spouse during the length of her pregnancy?"

Doug stood up. "Yes, but I'm not sure what that has to do with—"

"That's all I need to know. Sit back down." As soon as Doug took his seat, Barclay turned to Bailey. "I get that your circumstances are unusual, but I have to do what I feel is in the best interest of you and your child. Come see me after the baby is born. Divorce denied."

Nash heard her intake of breath from several feet away. "Wait, Judge Barclay!" She stepped toward the bench. "Please. I need this divorce. I can't stay married to Doug."

"Believe it or not, Ms. Hobbs, I'm doing you a favor. You need medical care for you and your child and, as his spouse, you are entitled to it under his insurance. I won't grant a divorce just to watch a young pregnant woman end up without medical coverage."

"But it's not Doug's child!"

"Doesn't matter. Unless the child's biological father has medical insurance and still wants to marry you, then there's nothing else I can do." The judge looked directly at Nash, as if offering him a cue, and then snickered. "Seems to me, you're more *his* wife than Mr. Smith's anyway…in every sense of the word."

Nash grinned. "And I *do* have insurance."

CHAPTER ELEVEN

BAILEY KNEW THE chance of the judge granting her divorce was slim to none the moment Nash opened his big mouth. By law, she was legally bound to disclose her pregnancy in a divorce case, but she wasn't showing yet, and most likely the judge wouldn't have asked her if she was pregnant. The divorce would've been finalized, and she would've been free from Doug forever.

But no. Nash ruined it by barging into the courtroom and demanding rights to a baby no one knew anything about. Not only did he have bad timing, but he also had home turf advantage, which hardly seemed fair.

She looked at his smiling face and narrowed her eyes. He was calm, too cool for her comfort. Whether he did this on purpose or not, Nash obviously knew he had her cornered. And once again, he was entertaining this stupid idea of marrying her to stay close to the baby.

The last thing she wanted was to rehash their previous argument or have a frank conversation about their iffy future in front of a group of strangers. There had to be a way to finesse her way out of the complicated dilemma she'd gotten herself into. But the smile he wore pissed her off.

"You think you have it all figured out, don't you?" she asked Nash, not bothering to hide her irritation.

"Hey, this hasn't been a walk in the park for me, either. But like I said, I think we could make it work. I want to try."

She crossed her arms and shook her head. "It's not going to happen."

Judge Barclay grinned, clearly amused by their unique circumstances. "Come on, Sutherland. You can do better than that.

I've seen you debate your way out of a paper bag. Why don't you state your case to Ms. Hobbs and see if you can't change her mind?"

"This is an outrage," Doug shouted. "I'm Bailey's husband. I think I should have a say as to—"

"Put a sock in it, Doug," the judge said, then motioned for Nash to go ahead.

Nash straightened his back, making himself look larger than he already was. His eyes zeroed in on her, and his lips formed a firm line. A muscle twitched in his cheek and his jaw tightened. He was serious. Dead serious. This was apparently his game face, one he probably used in court hundreds of times.

"Ms. Hobbs," Nash began, keeping a straight face and a professional tone. "Is there any question as to the paternity of your unborn baby?"

Bailey crossed her arms and tried not to laugh at his courtroom persona. "No," she said, playing along even though she thought it was pointless.

"For the record, can you please state who the biological father is of the child in question."

She rolled her eyes. "You."

"Let it be known that the witness has indicated Nash Sutherland as the father. Now, Ms. Hobbs..." He sauntered around the floor, pausing for dramatic effect. "What findings have led you to believe, beyond a reasonable doubt, that Mr. Sutherland would pose as a poor example of a husband?"

The question caught her off guard and she blinked. "Uh, nothing. It's just that—"

"So all parties agree that Mr. Sutherland would undoubtedly exercise all of his support obligations?"

"Well, yes...I guess, but—"

"Is it true that you are contemplating a move to a remote area of Alaska, a change in custodial setting that would deprive Mr. Sutherland of contact with his own child, a profound impact that surely would be in neither of their best interests?"

Several women in the room gasped and the bailiff shook his head in disapproval. Even Doug looked a little put out, which surprised her since that cheating dick obviously never gave a shit about anybody but himself. Bailey refused to answer Nash, figuring it was within her rights to plead the fifth. *Damn him. He's making me look like a jerk.*

Nash didn't wait for her response before he moved on with his questioning. "Is it true that you asked Mr. Sutherland to transfer custody to you, leaving the father with no parental rights whatsoever?"

Bailey sighed. This was getting out of hand. "Nash, that's enough."

Unfortunately, he didn't agree and continued. "Is it your position that Mr. Sutherland would not be a suitable father to your child and are suggesting to the court that he would be an unfit parent?"

Her eyes widened. "What? No! I didn't say that."

"So there's no question that Mr. Sutherland—"

"I object!" Bailey yelled. "And quit talking about yourself in third person. It's stupid."

Nash wore a proud grin, knowing damn well he had just won over everyone in the courtroom with his little speech. "Apparently, Ms. Hobbs would like the floor. I'd like to turn it over to her now…if it pleases the court."

"Oh, it does," Judge Barclay said with a chuckle. Then he caught the annoyed look Bailey gave him and cleared his throat. "Thank you, counselor. Ms. Hobbs? Is there anything you'd like to say in rebuttal?"

As all eyes turned to her, Bailey shifted nervously. She tried to think of an eloquent way to put her thoughts into words, but nothing would outdo Nash's stellar performance at making her look bad. After a long, thoughtful pause, she blurted out the only thing she could think of. "I cheat at board games."

Judge Barclay leaned toward the bailiff. "Well, hell, get the executioner on the line. We've got a stone-cold felon here."

Laughter rumbled throughout the courtroom.

"What I mean is…" She looked directly at Nash as the rumblings dissipated. "You don't know a thing about me. We're probably complete opposites and not the least bit compatible."

"Oh, I'd say we were plenty compatible…" Nash shrugged his eyebrows. Others in the room snickered, but he ignored them. He stepped closer and ran one strong finger down her cheekbone, then stroked her chin with his thumb. "I know it's not enough, but it's a damn good place to start, Bailey." His voice lowered considerably, as if he were speaking privately to her and a dozen other people weren't present. "You may not know me very well now, but you will."

Her breath hitched as a warm sensation coursed through her veins. It was the unspoken promise gleaming in his eyes that made his offer even more attractive. His bed would be the one place where they would get to know each other—really know each other—inside and out. Hell, it was more than Doug had ever offered her.

"But there's a minor glitch in your plan, Nash. We don't even like each other half the time. If you marry me, you'll only end up miserable."

The corners of his mouth lifted. "Haven't had a peaceful moment since I met you, anyway."

"I'm serious, Nash. We'll end up fighting like mortal enemies."

"Good. It'll give us a reason to have lots of make-up sex," Nash said with a serious, I'm-not-even-remotely-joking face.

Nash leaned on the judge's bench with one hand, waiting for her answer. He wore his sexy smirk, the one that could melt the panties off any woman within a five-mile radius. But that wasn't all Bailey saw in him. He was smart, funny, and cocky. And he looked hot. Really hot. God, no wonder he made her body want to ovulate. But she couldn't base her decision off her confused sensory glands.

She turned and addressed Judge Barclay. "Can I have a moment to myself, please?"

He nodded. "We'll adjourn for a short recess. Court will resume in fifteen minutes."

Bailey stepped out of the courtroom and looked for the nearest bathroom. She noted one at the end of the hallway and rushed inside, gasping in large breaths of fresh, Nash-free air. *Jesus. I was actually going to say yes. Am I fucking insane? This will never work.* The door opened behind her, but she didn't look up. Instead, she gripped the sink to keep her hands from shaking.

"Bailey?"

The sound of his voice startled her and she whirled around too fast, making herself dizzy. She braced herself against the paper towel dispenser. In a flash, Nash was there, holding her up, with one arm wrapped firmly around her waist as his concerned eyes stared into hers.

"Hey, what's wrong?"

She righted herself and wiggled out of his grip. "I-I'm fine. I was just a little dizzy, that's all. It's the morning sickness."

He wet a paper towel under the faucet and handed it to her. "If you're not feeling well, maybe you should sit down for a few minutes."

"No, really, I'm okay," she said, patting her forehead with the damp paper towel.

He rubbed at the back of her neck. "Well, as soon as I become your husband, you can let me focus on taking care of you and the baby for a while."

Her body stiffened. "Nash, about that…"

A coolness took over his face. "Don't do it. Don't back out on me now. You were going to say yes before you came in here and talked yourself out of it. I know you were. You were going to marry me."

She lowered her eyes, avoiding his gaze. "Not for the right reasons."

"Who gives a shit about the right reasons? Just marry me. All you have to do is say yes. We've already broken all the rules of dating, anyway. What's one more? The baby wants his parents to be together."

"There you go again, calling him a boy," she said, raising her voice. Nash quirked an eyebrow. *Shit. He's still got me doing it, too.* "Damn it, you know what I mean. And quit using our baby as a pawn. These tactics of yours aren't going to work."

"Well, if you weren't being so selfish, you'd see that—"

"Selfish? Are you fucking kidding me? I'm trying to keep you from making the biggest mistake of your life." She marched over to the trashcan and tossed her paper towel inside. "Damn it, Nash. Somewhere in this world, there is a woman you're meant to be with. *That* is the person you should want to marry."

Nash's eyes flared with anger. "And what makes you so goddamn sure that you're not her?" Then, without waiting for a response, he walked out the bathroom door, slamming it with an alarming amount of frustration.

A few minutes later, Bailey—feeling guiltier by the minute—emerged from the bathroom and sat outside the courtroom on a long wooden bench. She had five minutes before she needed to go back inside and wanted some time to clear her head before facing Nash for round two.

The door swung open and Judge Barclay stepped out. He held out his hands and offered her a package of peanut butter crackers and a bottle of water. "Sutherland said you were feeling sick. He ran down to the vending machine and got these for you."

"Thank you," she said, taking them from his hands. "But why are you bringing them out to me?"

"Guess he figures you wouldn't accept his help."

She frowned at that. "It's not that. It's just—"

"It's just that—and pardon my French—you're too plain chickenshit to take a chance on him."

"Excuse me?" Bailey said, blinking.

Barclay chuckled a little and sat down beside her, patting her knee. "Look, it's none of my business. But if you ask me, that boy is head over heels for you. I saw the way you two looked at each other in there. You've got chemistry."

"Maybe. But that isn't the same thing as love."

"No, it's better. Couples fall out of love all the time. It happens. But lust can keep you going for years. I should know…I married my wife two weeks after I met her and got her in the backseat of my Crown Victoria."

"You fell in love that quick?"

"Hell, no. I wanted to sleep with her some more. But the only way I was getting past her father or his shotgun was by marrying her. So I did. That was forty years ago."

Bailey smiled at him, though her heart and mind were still warring against each other. "Maybe we should go back inside."

"One more quick word of advice, Ms. Hobbs." Judge Barclay grinned and patted her hand. "Do me a favor. Shit or get off the pot already."

CHAPTER TWELVE

HE HAD NO right to be mad.

No matter how much he disagreed with her, he couldn't force her into marrying him. Deep down, Nash knew that. He even respected her decision to stand on her own two feet and not willingly participate in a loveless marriage. But it still pissed him off.

What is it about this woman that has me so unsettled? As the mother of his unborn child, of course he cared about what happened to her. But that wasn't it. Something else had him in an uproar. Something besides her being so damn frustratingly stubborn.

He looked up as she came in with the judge. She was carrying the bottle of water and the pack of crackers he had purchased to help with her morning sickness. He'd asked the bailiff to deliver them to her, but Barclay had volunteered instead. Nash wished she would just let him help her. She couldn't really want to raise this baby alone.

Damn it, she needs somebody. It may as well be me. But Bailey had made it perfectly clear that she didn't want him anywhere in the picture.

She stopped beside him, but he refused to look directly at her. He just wanted to quit delaying the inevitable. If Bailey would rather stay married to her cheating prick of a husband than be with him, then that was her choice and her loss. She'd have to live with the consequences.

As the judge took his seat behind the bench, the bailiff made his announcement. "All rise. Court is now in session. The honorable Judge Barclay is presiding."

"Okay, Ms. Hobbs," the judge said. "If there's nothing further I can do for you, then—"

"Wait. Give me a minute, please." She turned to Nash, and he glanced up to see her twisting her trembling fingers together and biting her lip. "Did you mean what you said?"

"About what?" he said, his tone coming out depressed and flat.

"In the bathroom, when you said I could be the woman you're meant to be with. Did you mean it?"

He nodded. "Of course I meant it. I wouldn't have said it if I didn't—"

"Then ask me again."

He stared deep into her eyes to see if they were talking about the same thing. "Ask you what exactly?"

She smiled, which was the only answer she gave.

"Are you sure, Bailey? I don't think I can stand to hear you say no again. There's only so much rejection a man can take."

"Ask me," she repeated.

His nerves twitched and his heart stopped beating, but he managed to force the words off his tongue. "M-marry me?"

Her smiled widened and her eyes softened, but there was no hesitation with her answer. "Yes."

Nash blinked, then reached for her, cupping his hand around the back of her neck and pulling her closer. "Really?"

She nodded, then laughed as he let out a whoop and wrapped his arms around her, swinging her in a circle. When he put her down, she looked a little green, but he couldn't stop grinning.

He pointed to the judge. "You heard that, right? She said she'd marry me."

Doug leaned back in his chair and mumbled, "So what. Been there, done that. And trust me, it's not all it's cracked up to be."

Nash started for him, but Bailey stepped in front of him, blocking his path. "He's just being an ass." She threw an ugly look over her shoulder at Doug and then glanced eagerly to the judge. "Now will you please grant the divorce?"

"You bet," he said with a proud smile. "Give me a minute to sign the divorce decree and make everything official."

Nash couldn't believe it. Maybe right now she was marrying him for the sake of the baby, but he hoped to turn that around. He didn't want that to be *why* they stayed married. Because he couldn't stand the thought of being anything but a hands-on father, he would make this marriage work. Not for the baby's sake, but for all their sakes. Of course, that was if she didn't back out before they made it down the aisle.

"When we're done here, why don't we go get some lunch and talk out the details?" Nash suggested. Then he cringed and ran his hand through his hair, realizing it sounded more like a business proposal. "What I mean is…"

"I know what you mean. And that's fine. I know we have a lot to discuss."

He nodded just as Judge Barclay called her name.

"Here's a copy of your divorce papers. They need to be filed first, but then you can go see Vickie over in the Vital Statistics office and take her this form and a copy of the final divorce decree. She'll help you from there."

"Vital statistics?" Nash asked. "Why does Bailey need to see Vickie? She didn't change her last name after she got married. Hobbs is her maiden name."

Judge Barclay let out a hard breath. "Sutherland, do you think I'm an idiot?"

"No, of course not. I just—"

"Texas law requires a person to wait thirty days after a divorce to remarry and there's a seventy-two hour waiting period after applying for a marriage license."

"I know, sir, but I'm not sure what either of those things have to do with Bailey."

Barclay grinned. "Surely you didn't think I'd trust her to carry out her end of the bargain on her own, did you? No offense, but Ms. Hobbs is a flight risk. I waived both waiting periods. I'll see you both back here at four o'clock."

"Hold on a second," Bailey said, her face bearing a confused look. "What happens at four o'clock?"

Nash's lips twitched a little, knowing she wasn't going to like what she was about to hear. "Our wedding."

CHAPTER THIRTEEN

"HE CAN'T DO this, can he?" Bailey asked, as she exited the courthouse with Nash and a marriage license in hand.

"Well, no. Not technically. But since it's Judge Barclay and he's about to retire, I'm pretty sure he thinks he can."

"Well, there's got to be some way we can get out of this." When Nash didn't respond, she realized he was no longer at her side and turned to see him standing frozen in the middle of the sidewalk, glaring at her. "What are you doing?"

"So you *were* planning on backing out of this marriage?"

"No, that's not what I meant. It's just all happening way too fast. I thought I'd have time to—"

"To what? Leave me high and dry while you run off to live in an igloo with *my* baby? I don't fucking think so."

Bailey waited for a lady to pass in front of her on the sidewalk before speaking. "Stop making a scene. I'm just saying it's a little quicker than what I had in mind. I thought maybe a trial run on living together under the same roof would weed out any complications that might arise between us. You know, like roomies or something. At least until we figured out how everything would work."

Nash stormed past, not bothering to wait for her. "Judge Barclay had you pegged—you *are* a damn flight risk. Sounds to me like you're hoping this doesn't work so you'll have an excuse to leave."

"That's not it at all. I'm just being realistic."

"No, you're being a coward. I didn't ask you to marry me because I wanted a goddamn roommate."

"Well, then what the hell *do* you want?"

He stalled and turned to face her. The storm brewing in his eyes forced her to take a step back. "You really want to know?"

She hesitated, then nodded slowly.

"What I want is to drive my cock so far inside you that you come until your eyes roll permanently into the back of your head. Then the last thing you're going to see me as is a fucking roommate. *That's* what I want."

Her mouth went dry. Most likely because it was hanging wide open. All she could say was, "Oh."

"That's all you've got to say?"

She opened her mouth to speak, but nothing came out, so she closed it again. *Yep. Apparently so.*

"Well, that's just great." He glanced at his watch. "You've got a little less than five hours to figure out what you're going to do. I'll be here at four o'clock. If you aren't, then I guess that tells me everything I need to know." Not bothering to wait for her response, Nash crossed the street and headed for his truck.

Bailey didn't even try to stop him. He seemed even more upset with her after she hadn't responded to his remark about what he wanted to do to her. But what the hell do you say to something so deliciously vulgar? *Okay? Yes, please? Is now a good time for you?* Because *that's* exactly what she wanted to respond with, though the words refused to leave her mouth.

That was probably a good thing, since she still hadn't decided on which course of action to take with this whole marriage business. And ending up back in Nash's bed before making that decision wouldn't be fair to either of them. No point in giving him false hope and toying with both of their emotions.

She couldn't deny that marrying Nash was an attractive offer. He was a good-looking, successful man who had a real interest in being a hands-on father to his child. That spoke volumes to his character. And she already knew what kind of lover he was. *Definitely no complaints in that department.* But what kind of husband would he be?

Would he be the kind of husband who brought her flowers and remembered their anniversary? Or would he be the type who became easily bored, and as soon as the newness of his favorite toy

94

wore off, he'd be looking for something—or someone—else to play with?

She hated to think that about him, but she had to consider it. Especially since her first husband hadn't been able to keep his dick in his pants even on his wedding night. She should have never married Doug. She knew that now. But if she were being honest, not everything had been his fault.

Something had been off in their relationship from the beginning, yet she'd ignored all the warning signs. Sure, Doug put on a great act most of the time, but when he proposed, it was the need for security and the desire to connect intimately with a man that ultimately led to her decision to say yes. And what a disaster that whole thing turned out to be.

The thought of paddling in circles, going from one marriage that wasn't meant to be into another, scared the hell out of her. But it also wasn't right to hold what Doug did to her over Nash's head.

Besides, he was nothing like Doug. Nash had made that perfectly clear when he'd saved her at the bar and again when he'd taken up for her inside the courtroom. He would be a protector, a friend, an everyday hero—for her, as well as the baby. But was that a good enough reason to enter into a marriage with him?

She wanted to give her child a better life than she'd had growing up with only one parent. But was this the solution? Bailey could raise this baby alone, but that didn't mean she wanted to. And Nash wasn't going to give up. No, he was a lawyer who was used to getting his way.

Clearly, Nash saw their marital arrangement as a foolproof plan, a chance to build a family and raise their child in a household with both parents, two people who would grow to love each other. Foolish expectations, if you asked her.

Skeptical as usual, Bailey knew their life together would be based on an adjustment period and a colorful assortment of complications in their new roles as husband and wife.

Then she imagined herself lying naked in Nash's bed with him hovering over her, pressing his hard muscled body into hers as he'd done before, and her stomach fluttered. *Good Lord. That's exactly what got us in this predicament to begin with.*

What she needed was perspective, which was exactly what a few hours away from Nash would give her. She had a decision to make.

And soon.

CHAPTER FOURTEEN

NASH LOOKED AT his watch again. 4:03. *Shit.*

The judge leaned over his desk. "Problem, Sutherland?"

"She's not coming, sir."

Judge Barclay leaned back in his chair comfortably. "She'll be here."

"It's after four. If she was planning on making an appearance, she would've been here already. I made it clear that if she pulled a no-show I'd take that as my answer." Nash's jaw clenched involuntarily. "And I guess I got one."

"Do you know nothing about women, son? They're almost always fashionably late, even to their own weddings. She'll be here."

Anger built inside Nash, stripping him of any lingering dignity. "Right, like you know anything about women. What are you on now, your fourth marriage?"

Judge Barclay pointed his gavel at Nash in a threatening manner. "I understand why you're upset, but don't forget whose courtroom this is. We may not be on a case, but I'll damn sure hold you in contempt if you speak to me like that again." Then he set his gavel down. "And keep that bit of information to yourself. Ms. Hobbs doesn't need to know about my failed marriages. I *may* have told her something a little different to give her some incentive to show up."

Nash lowered his head in resignation. "Look, I know Bailey didn't disclose her pregnancy to the court before her divorce proceedings like she was supposed to, but you're not really going to hold her in contempt and have her arrested if she doesn't show, are you?"

"Of course not. I don't throw pregnant women in jail. What kind of monster do you take me for?" Then he grinned and held his hands up in the air innocently. "Not my fault if Ms. Hobbs got that crazy idea in her head."

"She said you told her that."

"All hearsay…and you know we don't allow hearsay in my courtroom," Barclay said in a stern tone. "What happened between you two when you left here, anyway? You do something to change her mind?"

"We had words. But I didn't get to use nearly as many as she did."

The judge laughed. "Oh, hell, that's women for you. Can't live with them, can't shoot—"

The door flung open behind Nash, cutting off Barclay's words. Nash turned and blinked rapidly. Bailey stood there in a long, shimmery ivory gown. It wasn't a fancy dress—sort of plain, really—but the satin skimmed her curves in all the right places, and she'd pinned her wavy blonde locks back, allowing wispy pieces to fall and frame her delicate cheeks.

She wasn't smiling, though.

With her lips pursed and a look of determination on her face, Bailey marched forward, not stopping until she reached Nash's side. "If we're really going to do this, then let's get it over with."

"Oh, look, the blushing bride has arrived," Barclay announced.

Nash blinked again, still not believing what he was seeing. "Y-you came?"

She held out her arms. "Ta-da!" she said. "Now can we get a move on? I've got things to do if I'm going to uproot my entire life after marrying a complete stranger."

Her caustic tone made him frown. *Why is she so irritated?*

But before Nash could ask, the judge spoke up. "Bailiff, let in the witnesses."

"Witnesses?" Nash repeated, watching the bailiff make his way across the room to the adjoining doors for another courtroom.

The judge smiled. "Everyone in the courtroom this morning wanted to see how all this played out, and since I figured you two yahoos wouldn't think about bringing your own witnesses…well, let's just say I'm providing them for you. I ordered them to wait in the empty courtroom next door, just in case Ms. Hobbs decided not to show." He lowered his tone and mumbled, "Didn't want to embarrass you, Sutherland."

Nash gave him a disgruntled snort. "Thought you said she *would* show?"

"Well, she's here, isn't she?"

The bailiff opened the doors and a crowd began flooding into the room, staring and smiling at Nash and his bride-to-be. Apparently, he wasn't the only one who was surprised she'd showed up.

"Wait a minute," Bailey said, as people filled the seats. "There weren't *this* many people here earlier today."

"Instant celebrity status," Judge Barclay said, smiling. "Word travels fast in the courthouse."

"Oh, that's just great." Bailey looked at Nash with her lips in a tight, thin line and shook her head in disgust.

"Why are you looking at me like that?" he asked. "I didn't have anything to do with this."

"Yes, you did! This is all *your* fault. If you hadn't burst into the courtroom earlier today and caused such a big scene, then none of this would've happened."

"Why don't you two argue about this later," Barclay intervened, giving them both a terse nod. "We've got a ceremony to start." He picked up some papers from his desk, cleared his throat, and began to read from them. "Ladies and gentlemen, today we have gathered to celebrate the marriage of…"

The judge continued talking, but Nash couldn't take his eyes off Bailey long enough to pay attention. As soon as the judge started reading from the script, her heated expression dissolved into a murky puddle and all the blood drained from her face. Her stiff posture held her position remarkably well for someone who looked ready to hit the floor.

She smoothed out the satin material of her dress over and over again, like she wasn't sure what to do with her hands, until they fluttered over her stomach and stayed there. That move cracked his heart into two jagged pieces. Without saying a word, he knew what she was thinking. *I'm doing this for the baby.*

And he was thinking the same thing. The only difference was that he was sure as time passed, they'd grow to care and love each other in the way a husband and wife should. Bailey, on the other hand, didn't seem so sure about that.

But what could he do? Give up his child by letting her leave? *Not a chance in hell.* No, *he* would make this marriage work, no matter what it took. With or without Bailey's cooperation. All he had to do was make her happy. Now if he could just figure out how the hell to do that without screwing everything up.

"Sutherland!" the judge said, raising his voice.

Nash shook his head, clearing his thoughts, and forced himself back to reality. "What?" he snapped back.

"Get your head out of your ass. I asked you a question."

"Oh. Uh, yes. I mean, I do."

The judge cut his eyes to the woman at Nash's side. "Bailey Marie Hobbs, will you take Nash William Sutherland, to be your lawful wedded husband? Will you grow to love, comfort, honor, and protect him; forsaking all others until death do you part?"

Her shaking hand moved to her throat, and she hesitated as her gaze flitted to an empty glass pitcher on a nearby table. With no water in sight, she finally squeaked out, "I...d-do."

The judge grinned. "We'll skip the part with the rings and move on to—"

"Actually," Nash interrupted, pulling a small ring box from his pocket and opening it. "I stopped off at the jeweler's on the way here, just in case."

Inside the black box was a duo of platinum rings set in black velvet: a woman's three-carat diamond wedding band and a man's thicker, contoured band.

Bailey's glistening eyes widened, filling with tears, as her mouth dropped open. The shocked, appreciative look on her face sent a thrill through Nash, warming his heart and loosening the knot in his stomach. He'd wanted to make her feel special, and her expression led him to believe he'd done just that.

The judge smiled as Nash placed the box on his bench and pulled out the diamond ring. "Nice touch, Sutherland," Barclay said with a wink. "Now repeat after me..."

Nash captured Bailey's trembling hand in his and gave it a light squeeze to help calm her nerves. She smiled softly as he slid the sparkling band up her left ring finger and repeated the words given to him by the judge. "With this ring, I thee wed, and with it, I bestow all the treasures of my mind, my heart, and my hands."

Bailey blushed a little, but reached for the other ring, pulling it from its box and did the same. Her words weren't nearly as smooth, and she hadn't looked directly into his eyes as she spoke them, but the way her slender fingers rubbed across the top of his hand in a soothing motion was enough. Even a gesture as small as her slight touch was enough to convince Nash that this would work.

"Today you came here as individuals, but you will leave here as a couple. By the power enthroned in me, by the state of Texas, I now pronounce you husband and wife. Counselor, you may now kiss your bride."

Before Nash had a chance to move, Bailey leaned up on her toes and quickly brushed her lips across his. It happened so fast that Nash stood there in silence, wearing the same frown as everyone else.

"I think we can do better than that," he said, stepping toward her. She backed up, flickering a gaze at the witnesses. But Nash didn't care that they had an audience.

"Bailey, you're my wife now, and I'm going to kiss you as such." He took another step forward, determined to end this never-ending battle of wills between them.

She didn't move away this time. Instead, she lifted her stubborn chin and put up a hand to stop him from reaching out to her. "Hold up, Prince Charming. I may be your wife now, but that doesn't mean you're going to do whatever you want with me. Don't make me get a protective order against you already."

The judge chuckled under his breath.

Nash glared at him until he stifled his laughter and then turned back to Bailey. "That's not the way this is going to go," he said, grasping her arms and pulling them to his chest. "I'm going to kiss you properly, and I don't give a damn who's watching."

Threading his fingers into her soft hair, he bent slowly and touched his lips to hers with a gentle, firm pressure. He eased her into the kiss, but the moment she relaxed and opened her mouth a little, he pressed further, running his tongue along her bottom lip. With their eyes still open, Nash witnessed the panic flashing through hers as a breathless sigh escaped her mouth.

It nearly undid him. *The mother of his unborn child. His woman. No, his wife. And she was responding to him.*

He let go of her arms and snaked his around her waist, pulling her close enough that he could smell the perfume of her hair and feel her rapid heartbeat pounding against his chest. Nash meant to end it there. He really did. But it was impossible to be this close to her and not want to ravish her completely.

One more taste. That's all I need.

His tongue slipped between her dry, parted lips, seeking another response. Initially, she shied away, but then settled into the kiss as her tongue tentatively touched his in return. For Nash, it was like metal striking flint. What started as a spark, quickly grew into a roaring fire inside of him, and he realized that he was wrong. *One taste will never be enough.*

It wasn't graceful. Hell, it wasn't even decent.

As a prisoner of his own desire, Nash lost his wits and allowed his male libido to take over. His hands moved to her slim neck, anchoring her in place, as he covered her mouth with his, putting his heart and soul into the kiss. No warning. No negotiations.

Bailey clung helplessly to his broad shoulders, seemingly disabled by his dominance and his strong demand for submission. She kissed him back, within reason, but disciplined herself. For a moment, Nash didn't understand her reluctance, but then he realized his lapse in judgment.

An entire room of people are watching us make out. Shit.

Nash loosened his grip and harnessed his fervor.

They weren't alone...*yet.*

He wiped his thumb over her wet, swollen bottom lip and studied her curiously. She may have held back, but she damn sure hadn't tried to stop him. Her half-closed eyes held a content, glazed look, and her hair was slightly disheveled. It was a dick-hardening reminder of how she'd looked in his arms once before when he'd given her the first memorable orgasm she'd ever...

Whoa! Wait a minute. She's never been intimate with another man. Would she regret that as time went on? But the image of another man putting his hands on her, touching what was now his, pissed him off in a way he hadn't imagined. Nash decided right then and there that he was okay with him being her one and only, and would make damn sure she never regretted it for a second. Then his mouth twitched into a full-on smile.

That alone must've snapped Bailey out of the euphoric fog she was in. She glanced around and took in their audience. Her cheeks reddened and her face warped into a scowl as she pushed him away from her. "Okay, that's it. I want a divorce."

Nash felt his grin reach his eyes. "Tough shit."

The judge chuckled. "Ladies and gentlemen, I present to you Mr. and Mrs. Sutherland."

CHAPTER FIFTEEN

AFTER HANGING UP with her father, Bailey hadn't felt much like talking. He'd chastised her—like she'd figured he would—but he'd also given the two of them his blessing. Then he'd promised her that everything would work out in the end.

If only she could be sure of that herself.

"How are you feeling?" Nash asked.

Bailey knew this was coming. She'd been staring out the truck's passenger window for the last five minutes, completely mute, while watching the trees blur past. She cut her eyes to him. "You know how it feels when everything in your life seems to be going right?"

He smiled and nodded.

"Yeah, the opposite of that." Then she went back to staring out the window.

Nash cleared his throat. "You seem a bit grouchy."

"I wonder why," she said, sarcastically. "Maybe it has something to do with my new husband being a complete stranger. Or maybe how my entire life shifted just to suit him."

"Come on, Bailey. You had to give up your apartment. I wasn't living apart from my pregnant wife."

"No, it's not the apartment." She turned back to look at him. "I'm talking about how you gave all my stuff to the landlord and told him to have a moving sale. You had no right." She folded her arms across her chest.

"Hey, I told you to go through and point out anything you wanted to keep first. You could've taken more than just your clothes and toiletries. That was *your* decision. There was plenty of room in my truck for more of your belongings. And if you had wanted to keep some of your furniture, all you had to do was say something."

"You already have furniture and...well, it's nicer than mine."

Nash glanced over at her, probably wanting to see if she looked as embarrassed as she sounded. Apparently, she did. "I'll buy us some brand new furniture," Nash said. "You can pick it out."

She sighed. "You don't have to do that."

"It's not a big deal," he said, shrugging. "Besides, we have to go car shopping next week, anyway. While we're out, we'll hit up a few furniture stores."

"I already told you that I'm not letting you buy me a car...even if you did sell mine to my neighbor for a lousy three hundred dollars."

"That car was a piece of shit. You were driving around in a ticking time bomb."

"What are you talking about? That was a good-running car."

He shook his head. "No, you said it broke down on you three times in the last few weeks."

"It did. But this week, it was running okay."

Nash chuckled. "The check engine light was on, the transmission was slipping, and the seats looked like they were mauled by a cougar. If anything, I should've *paid* that guy three hundred dollars to have the damn car crushed. And yes, I am buying you a new one."

"No. You're not." *Why does he keep insisting on spending money? I still owe him for the doctor visit. Jeez.* "I don't really have anywhere to go, anyway. I quit my job, remember? Doctor appointments are the only thing I'll have to go to, and I can call a cab."

"Like hell!" Nash gripped the steering wheel tighter as he turned onto the caliche-paved driveway. "*I'm* taking you to all your appointments. I want to be a part of everything having to do with this child, including the doctor visits."

Bailey blinked, not knowing what to say to that. *He wants to be part of everything where the baby's concerned...but what about me?* So, she went back to the original argument. "Well, that only proves my point. I don't need a car."

Nash shook his head again, which was his only response. The sun dipped behind the trees as they pulled up the drive and parked in front of the red brick ranch house that Bailey would now call home.

She stepped out, surveying the large plot of land, until her gaze fell on the large wooden corral attached to the barn. Three horses stood in parade fashion at the white fence, heads hanging over the top rail while their ears twisted back and forth.

"Oh, we have horses."

Nash joined her at the front of the truck. "You didn't notice them the last time you were here?"

"Of course I did, but I didn't think I'd ever see…" She bit her lip.

"Go ahead and say it," he said in a frustrated tone. "If I hadn't found you when I did, you'd never have come back here, much less told me about the baby." When she didn't respond, he added, "Well, it's true, isn't it?"

She hesitated, then whispered a soft, "Yes."

He winced at her honesty. "Then it's a good thing I found you when I did. And just for the record, it's not like I asked you to leave. You left that morning before I woke up." His eyes met hers. "Can I assume that your days of sneaking out on me are over?"

"Without a car, a job, or an apartment, where else would I go?" *Oh, great. Now I feel like a stray dog that followed him home, hoping like hell he'll throw me a bone.* She shrugged it off, though, and offered him a cheeky grin. "Guess you're stuck with me for now."

"I was hoping you'd say that, but next time leave off the *for now.*" A slow smile spread on his face. "I told you before, I don't believe in divorce. I meant it."

Before she could fully register what he said, her legs were swept out from under her and he lifted her into his arms. Startled by the sudden movement, Bailey latched her limbs around his neck and held on as he carried her into the house. He didn't put her down until they made it to the living room.

Nash gave her a wink. "Welcome home, darlin'."

A flash of heat simmered in her body at the term of endearment. But she shook it off. *He probably calls every woman that. It doesn't mean anything.* "You didn't have to carry me over the threshold. I know it's traditional, but there's nothing traditional about our…er, arrangement. Besides, I still have to get my suitcases out of the truck."

"I'll get them." He moved toward the door. "Just relax and make yourself at home."

"Um, Nash…?"

He paused before walking out. "Yeah."

"Which bedroom is mine?"

"Last door on the right."

"But…isn't that *your* room?" she asked, squinting at him.

A smirk settled on his stoic face, but he didn't say anything. He just winked and continued his lazy stroll out to the truck. Bailey stood there a second longer, absorbing the evasive response and dissecting the hidden meaning until… *Oh. My. God.*

He'd walked out so calm. As if he hadn't just pointed out that he had every intention of honoring his husbandly role. She hadn't expected to take up residence in his bed the very first night. *Christ. Now what do I do?*

Okay, in all fairness, Nash *had* said this wouldn't be a cardboard-constructed marriage and she'd be his wife in every sense of the word. But so soon? Wouldn't he want to get to know her better first? Find out what kind of person she was? *God, I'm such an idiot! Of course he wouldn't. This is the same guy who took me home five minutes after meeting me.*

And, if she were being honest, she wasn't any better. It wasn't like she had put up much of a fight. In fact, when Nash wanted her legs up in the air, she hadn't hesitated to ask him how high. Because turning down a man like Nash was nearly impossible…virgin or not.

She blew out a hard breath.

The thought of recapturing the intimacy of that first night with Nash—this time as his wife—was enough to send nervous energy zinging under her skin. Not only because she was enthusiastic about getting reacquainted, but mainly because she felt like a complete stranger to her own husband.

But why should that matter? They *were* complete strangers before and it didn't seem to bother either of them.

Then it hit her.

The night was based on a one-night-stand and wasn't supposed to mean anything. A frisky romp in the sack that ended there. No feelings. No further communication. No strings. But, even then, it was never quite that.

This time would be different, the stakes much higher. And *that* scared the shit out of her. Nash had already proven that, physically, he could destroy her. But this time the destruction would be emotional. *No, I can't let that happen. Especially not with Nash.*

He could hurt her so much more than Doug ever had. Even before Nash had shown up on her doorstep that first day, she hadn't stop thinking about him. She'd felt things with him that she'd never knew existed. Maybe it was because he was the first man she'd ever let get close enough to touch her, to reach inside her and pull out sensations that she'd never felt before. She doubted that her ex—or any other man, for that matter—could've made her feel the same way. Doug may have hurt her, but Nash would be the one to shatter her.

Damn it.

If only she could laminate her heart to keep Nash from getting inside; seal the edges to keep the emotions from seeping through. Maybe then, she'd manage to keep her sanity when he threw her out the door on her ass and engaged her in a nasty custody battle. Because *that* was exactly what she saw happening the moment the baby arrived.

But how do I keep myself on level ground where Nash is concerned? It's not like I can just avoid him.

Realistically, she couldn't gracefully bow out of having a sexual relationship with her own husband, could she? Especially when she wanted him to touch her, to make her feel like she had the night he'd wrapped her legs around his waist and ridden her to ecstasy. Something he'd done more than once that evening as she recalled.

Just thinking about it made her thighs involuntarily clench together and her entire body warmed considerably.

Through the open door, she saw Nash making his way back to the house, luggage in hand. It filled her with an enormous amount of unneeded anxiety, so Bailey hurried down the hallway toward his bedroom. She didn't want to face him until she had herself straightened out and more under control.

Any guilt she felt over retreating to the bedroom was quickly snuffed out by one glaring fact: Nash didn't love her. It was just sex to him, plain and simple. She was an incubator for his unborn child, that's all. And no matter what Nash said, Bailey knew that once the baby arrived, all bets were off.

Sooner or later, he would realize the mistake he'd made and opt out of this loveless marriage. *See? I'm worrying for nothing. Nash doesn't look at me as anything more than a piece of ass who's harboring his offspring.*

She opened the bedroom door and gasped.

The room itself was the same as she remembered: dark marine blue walls matching the plush comforter on the king-sized bed, hardwood floors with cherry wood furniture, and a muted grey upholstered chair that sat in front of two large windows framed by the same color drapes. A sophisticated, masculine bedroom with a clash of bold hues and neutral tones.

But that wasn't why she was taken aback. Nope. It was the random, various things in the room meant to inspire romantic feelings that had her ready to keel over. Dimmed lights. Lit candles. Soft music. And the long-stemmed red rose laying on the bed, attached to a small card by a thin satin ribbon.

She moved closer, lifted it, and read it to herself. *Sweetheart, thank you for showing up and giving us a chance to bloom. Together, we will make this work. Your husband.*

She wanted to find fault with it. A spelling or punctuation error. Something. Anything. But it was kindest, most thoughtful thing any man had ever done for her, which demonstrated what kind of man she'd married. *This is his way of telling me he isn't playing house and his vows mean something to him. But can I trust that?*

A sudden queasiness settled inside her as she became aware of him standing behind her. He was silent, but she sensed him. Like static electricity. She couldn't see him, but her hair stood on end, giving her a weird sensation that something was touching her. It had to be his eyes. She could almost feel them burning through her like the pinpoint of a laser.

Then he came into view as he crossed the room, his boots clacking lightly on the wooden floor beneath his feet. He stopped in front of the nightstand, opened the drawer, and withdrew an envelope that he laid on the bed in front of her. "I thought you might like to know I got tested shortly after our last encounter. My results came back clean."

She gasped. "Y-you thought I gave you something—"

"No, of course not," he said easily. "When I eventually found you, I'd planned to show you that you had nothing to worry about. I always try to be responsible for my actions—sexually or otherwise—so this was my assurance to you that I hadn't given *you* anything."

"Oh."

"If you don't mind, I'm going to get out of these dress clothes and slip into something more comfortable," he said, pulling at his tucked-in shirt. Bailey couldn't speak past the knot in her throat, so she only nodded, which made Nash grin. "By the way, in case you were wondering, I haven't been with anyone since that night, either."

Working from the top down, Nash unbuttoned his pressed white shirt and slid it off his shoulders, revealing impressive abs and firm pectoral muscles. His biceps flexed as he tossed the shirt into the hamper in the corner. When he turned back, her gaze drifted to the small trail of hair leading into the tight jeans that clearly outlined a glorious hard-on.

Bailey bit into her bottom lip. She knew from personal experience that the only thing sexier than Nash without a shirt was Nash without pants. She closed her eyes, avoiding the visual impact of his half-naked form. It was bad enough that she'd never get the image of the fully-nude version of him out of her head. She didn't need to torture herself more.

"God, I love when you do that."

Her eyes flicked open. "What?"

"That. What you're doing right now."

Inevitably, her fingers had touched her lips, soothing her frazzled nerves. She dropped her hand to her side and forced it to stay there. "I do that when I get—"

"Nervous?"

"I was going to say uncomfortable."

He unbuttoned his jeans, then paused, his eyes meeting hers briefly. "Do I make you *uncomfortable*?"

CHAPTER SIXTEEN

⸺⟡⸺

NASH GRINNED AT the way her cheeks reddened before she could turn away. "No, I… It's just a bad habit," she said quickly.

He approached her from behind, his broad shoulders towering over her smaller ones, as his figure blocked the light of the candles on the dresser behind them, creating a shadow over her.

Her perfume filled the air around her. The light, flowery fragrance was a subliminal reminder of their first night. They hadn't been together since, but he had spent the last six weeks thinking about nothing else. The way his hands had roamed her body, looking for ways to heighten her pleasure with every touch. His mouth had traveled every inch of her skin, tasting and consuming her endlessly. And his fingers… *Jesus. The things I'd done to her with my fingers.*

Nash moved closer, his hard length pressing into her fully, as his lips brushed her ear lobe. "I looked for you," he whispered, placing his large hands on her hips and feeling her quiver beneath them. "Every day. For over a month, I searched for your face in every crowd. It drove me nearly crazy until…" He hesitated, breathing out heavily, but slanted his body more firmly into hers.

She leaned back against him, allowing the warmth of his body to leach into hers. "Until what?" she asked softly, her breath hitching.

"I gave up, Bailey. I figured I wasn't ever going to find you, so I stopped looking and went to Rowdy's. It was the first time I'd been back there since the night we met. I was going to plow myself with enough alcohol to make me forget all about you. I needed to get you out of my head. But halfway through my second beer, the waitress saw me and asked me about my lady friend…the one who'd stormed out and left her credit card behind. That's why it took me so long to find you. But just when I'd given up, it was like fate stepped in and intervened on our behalf."

"W-why are you telling me this?"

His tone became more serious. "Because I want you to know what you're getting yourself into. I'm not stupid, Bailey," he said, anger lacing his words. "I can feel the gears grinding in your head, trying to figure out a way to keep me at a safe distance. I won't let you do it. Not when I know we're meant to be. I didn't go through all of this for nothing."

"Nash, I…" She tried to turn around to face him, but his hands on her waist tightened their grip, stilling her motion.

"If you give yourself to me now, I get all of you. There's no going back. I mean it."

He released her, walked past the bed, and plopped down in the upholstered chair to remove his boots. She winced as he chucked the first one on the floor. He hadn't meant to get angry, but he had no doubt what he said was true. She was planning on holding back and not allowing herself to become attached. He saw the fear of it in her eyes and the way she tensed under his hands.

But what he was offering her wasn't a sexual arrangement. He expected an emotional connection to his wife as much as a physical one, but that was just a symbol of what he was truly asking of her. In actuality, he wanted the one thing she probably would refuse to give him.

Trust.

He imagined just the thought of putting her faith in another man left her mouth dry and her head spinning with insecurities. Could she conquer her fears and let go of the doubts she had about this marriage? Would that be enough for them to make it work? Or would he only be setting himself up for heartbreak when she ran out on him?

Again.

Nash leaned back in the chair, watching her intensely. He made it clear he was waiting for a response. He wanted to exude confidence and warmth, but knew the determination he planted on his face would force her to make a decision. Because he wasn't making a move until he received an answer to his unasked question: *Will you allow me to earn your trust?*

There was a vulnerability in her eyes he'd never seen before. She was scared to death and examining her options. Not that he'd left her many. It was their wedding night, and he needed to know if she was willing to give this marriage a shot. A real one.

Years of being in a courtroom had taught him persuasion, but he wanted her to make this decision on her own. She needed to decide for herself if she was willing to take a chance on him, on them. But that didn't mean he couldn't offer her a helping hand.

He held out his palm. "Well?"

Bailey hesitated, but then accepted it. When he pulled her into his lap, she gave him a half-hearted smile. "Don't hurt me," she whispered.

Her words wounded him, cutting him deep. He knew what it cost her to say it out loud and hated how weak her voice sounded. "I wasn't planning on it," Nash said, gliding his fingers behind her neck.

He wanted to comfort her, assure her that he was the kind of man who deserved her trust, but telling her that wasn't going to be enough. He needed to earn her trust. And that was exactly what he planned to do.

Nash pulled her closer and slowly brushed his mouth across hers, stopping for only a second to nibble lightly on her full lips. When she opened to allow him further access, Nash took the kiss to a deeper level and flexed his tongue against hers. Bailey melted into him, combing her fingers lightly through the hair at the back of his neck as he ran his in a straight line down her back, loosening the ties of her satin dress.

Impatiently, he pulled the dress down to her waist as she slid her arms out, leaving a pretty white bra covering her pert breasts. Nash nipped gently at one of the stiff peaks poking through the lacy fabric. Bailey shivered, and he raised an eyebrow.

"Sensitive," Bailey explained, blushing a little as she reached back and removed her bra and let it fall down to the floor. "Because of the pregnancy, I guess."

Nash raised one brow, then dropped his gaze to the rosy nubs before him. He thumbed over the other one with a light touch and she quivered once again. "Hmm. Interesting," he said, then lowered his mouth to see if his tongue could cause the same reaction.

She squirmed in his lap until she couldn't take it anymore. But he was glad they stopped when they did. The way she wiggled wildly over his erection—even through the layers of clothing—had his dick aching to get at her. But he wasn't ready for that. Not yet.

He lifted her off him and stood, grasping the material around her waist. Then he shoved it down past her hips, exposing her white satin panties and allowing the dress to puddle around her feet. She stepped out of it, kicked off her heels, and started to remove her panties when Nash stopped her.

"Leave them on," he commanded, motioning to the upholstered chair. "And sit down."

She did as he asked, but wrinkled her brow. She didn't seem to understand what he was doing. Not until he lowered himself in front of her and spread her legs wider. He peppered soft kisses over her thighs, then allowed his tongue to lightly trail upward until he reached the silky barrier.

He pressed his tongue firmly against the sleek undergarment, directly over her clit, and lapped at her repeatedly. As the smooth panties raked against her core, she moaned louder and louder. Nash grinned inwardly as he continued to pleasure her. He prided himself on being innovative in the bedroom, almost as much as he did in the courtroom.

Her heated flesh pulsated beneath the wet fabric and her thighs trembled. But the moment she began to buck, Nash gripped her hips tightly and slid two fingers under her satin panties, working them inside her. She fisted his hair as her inner muscles clamped down on his fingers and her body strained against his mouth.

When her energy stores depleted and the quivers subsided, Nash eased his fingers out of her and backed away, not allowing himself to touch her again so soon. Surely she would be sensitive all over.

Besides, he didn't trust himself to let her fully recover before he bent her over the chair and took her in an animalistic fashion. And that wasn't what he wanted for her on her wedding night.

He was eager to get inside her, but he wanted to make love to her, not go for instant gratification. He was already on the edge and knew he wouldn't last more than a minute after watching all the erotic faces she'd pulled as she came on his tongue.

No woman had ever made him feel so weak, so out of control of his own body, but he needed to show her that she was in competent, capable hands.

If only I can get my fucking hands to quit shaking.

CHAPTER SEVENTEEN

BAILEY WAS AFRAID to open her eyes, for fear that she wouldn't like the expression on his face. *Did he leave?* "Nash…?"

"I'm here, sweetheart."

She let out a small sigh. "Is something wrong?"

"I just…need a minute." His voice sounded strained.

Bailey wasn't sure what to make of that. One minute, he had her seeing prisms of color from the powerful orgasm he gave her, and the next, her mind was wiped clean, worrying that he had a change of heart. *Why else would he pull away?*

She opened her eyes and gazed at him. He was kneeling before her, head down, and breathing almost as heavily as her. "If you want to stop, I'll understand."

His head shot up, and his heated eyes met hers dead-on. But there wasn't regret or rejection in them. Only hot desire, blazing through like a melting pot about to boil over. She remembered that look from their first time together.

"I don't," he assured her, rising quickly.

Bailey stiffened as Nash slid his hands under her, gently lifted her into his arms, and turned to lay her on the bed. Then he walked over to the dresser and blew out the candles one by one, leaving behind the faint scent of vanilla-infused smoke. Moonlight filtered through the open curtains as Nash removed his jeans and reached into the nightstand drawer, pulling out a condom.

"You don't have to," she said softly. "It's not like I'm going to get pregnant or something."

He paused, then dropped it back into the drawer before climbing on the bed and crawling up between her legs. He leaned forward on his forearms, holding himself above her while not allowing his weight to press into her. "Are you sure?"

In answer, she pulled his mouth to hers.

Nash kissed her deeply, while shifting himself into position at her entrance. The moment he nudged against her, she knew he had a hardcore super erection, one she instantly wanted inside her. *Guess he really hadn't wanted to stop, after all.*

He claimed her slowly, sinking into her inch by inch until he was seated deeply inside her. He stilled himself briefly, his eyes closed and his jaw held taut. "You okay?" he asked, while holding himself completely still.

Maybe I should ask him the same thing. "Yes," she whispered. There was a slight discomfort on her end, but she knew it would be over the moment he started moving.

And she was right.

Nash started slow with small thrusts, easing in and out of her in varying rhythms and alternating his motions. But even as he picked up speed, he still wasn't doing so with the pizzazz he possessed the last time they were together. *Was he afraid of hurting her? Or the baby?* She thought she remembered reading somewhere about men who had an irrational fear of hurting their unborn child in the womb during sex.

She tried to match his thrusts and encouraged him to become more assertive, but he seemed motivated to continue at his current pace. Like he was messing with her, letting her slowly go mad beneath him, yet purposely dedicated himself to keeping her from flying off the orgasmic cliff.

The closer she got to the edge, the more he backed off. As if he didn't care that she was way past critical and well overdue for another orgasm. And how the hell was he still going so long? She felt like they'd been screwing for damn near an eternity. *Just great. I married the fucking Energizer Bunny.*

As urgency set in once again, she became more persistent, clawing at his back, feeling his dense muscles under her nails. She panted steadily, becoming more frazzled by the minute, a feeling she struggled to communicate. "Nash," she pleaded. "I...I need to..."

She caught the sexy curve of his lips. "No, this is what you need," he said, lowering his mouth to her ear as his voice softened. "You need your husband to make love to you."

Ah, so that's what he was doing: making love to his wife. All the extra attention he paid to the room's details and consideration for her enjoyment was some sort of courting ritual. He was patiently worshipping her body to show her that this wasn't just a fling. Not that she was complaining, but at least now it all made sense.

"If you liked what I did to you earlier, you're going to love this." Then he covered her mouth with his and slid one hand between them, touching her in just the right spot.

Remembering the sensations he'd already given her and feeling the new sensations he created within her, Bailey sighed against his lips. *Oh, God, his mouth…and fingers.*

He pulled back again, his eyes flitting across her face. "I'm going to watch you come while I'm inside you. Ready?"

She blinked, fully alert, not knowing what the hell he was talking about. Ready? No, she wasn't ready. She was…earlier. But he kept pulling her back from the brink. *I can't possibly have an orgasm on command. Can I?*

A smile played on his lips as he tilted his body more into hers, allowing himself deeper access. He obviously did so with a purpose. If it wasn't her imagination, he seemed to be seeking…something. As if he was a pirate, searching her depths for lost treasure. He wore an unnerving stare and focused all his attention on maintaining the position until he found what he so diligently sought after.

Gradually, a slow flame sparked inside her, spreading warmth across her abdomen as it grew. Her vocalizations must've clued him in that he'd struck gold because his grin widened, and although he continued at the same enhanced angle, his thrusts strengthened, growing alarmingly fast in speed.

Her hand slid across the smooth sheets, clutching them in an effort to hang on to something tangible. Nash had ignited a fire inside her that made his every stroke more intricate, more vibrant. Then it became an incinerator until finally the ball of flames combusted, causing her toes to curl as she released a guttural moan.

Hell, if she could've remembered his name, she would've screamed it.

Holy shit. It does exist.

Nash had hit a magic button somewhere inside her with precision and accuracy, and had just gifted her the ultimate orgasm. And her inner spasms had triggered his own grunting release.

When the erotic vibrations finally faded and the crippling sensations had evaporated, all that was left was a lingering heat between them. He held himself over her, staying entirely too still for her comfort, and panting heavily. His eyes stared down at her. Dreamy eyes that looked like ice crystals in the moonlight.

Damn it, Nash. I can't fall for you. I just can't.

So she looked away.

After a moment of silence, he sighed and collapsed on the bed beside her, draping a light arm over her waist. "Rest while you can. In a few minutes, we're going to do it all over again."

Her head snapped back to him. "We're what?"

"You heard me. And we're going to keep on doing it until you stop pulling away from me."

Holy hell. He's worse than the Energizer Bunny!

CHAPTER EIGHTEEN

NASH HADN'T MEANT to overwhelm her. But he damn sure wasn't going to apologize for making love to his wife all night long. It was their wedding night, after all. And well, frankly, she could've said no. *Thank God she didn't.*

A slow smile curved his lips. Nope, she hadn't refused him at all.

In fact, she'd been more than willing to participate in the rest of the night's events. By the time the sun rose above the horizon, Nash lay tangled in the sheets, completely relaxed, with Bailey curled into his chest and sleeping like a baby.

A very loud, snoring baby.

And that was when she wasn't sounding eerily like a deep-sea scuba diver. But even that, Nash found to be an endearing quality because somehow this woman had already sunk her claws deep into him.

It hadn't happened last night, though. No, if he were being honest, his interest in her had peaked the night he met her. From the very beginning, Bailey had tripped him up in the bar, figuratively speaking, and he'd been falling ever since.

Somehow, she'd branded her name on his heart. He didn't normally believe in love at first sight, but this damn sure felt like the same thing. And every touch, every cry of pleasure from last night's lovemaking had only confirmed what he already suspected. *I'm already falling for her.*

But that wasn't something he could tell her. Not yet, anyway. He'd spent the entire night keeping her focused on him and the sinful things he'd done to her body. Until she stopped pulling away—emotionally and physically.

He wasn't about to do anything to jeopardize the ground he'd gained with her in such a short period of time. Knowing her, she'd run for the hills. Not only because she wouldn't believe him, but because, to her, they were just empty promises. His intention was to prove to her that he meant every single word.

Starting right now.

It was the first day of the rest of their lives together and his new wife was lying in his arms. Nothing could ruin this moment for them.

"Nash," a muted voice called out.

Shit. Except her.

He slipped out of bed and yanked on a pair of jeans. Bailey stirred, but didn't wake up. Silently, he crept out the door and closed it softly behind him. The aroma of his favorite imported coffee grew stronger as he made his way down the hall, following the sounds of pots and pans clattering in the kitchen.

His mother stood in front of the counter, fork in hand, whisking eggs together in a white ceramic bowl. Bacon sizzled in the frying pan on the stove next to her, and through the glass door on the oven, he noted rising biscuits were already starting to brown.

Sonofabitch. How long has she been here?

He leaned against the door jamb and ran his fingers through his hair. "What are you doing here, Mom?"

She glanced over her shoulder and smiled at him. "Can't a mother visit her only son and make him breakfast?"

Nash snorted. "Dad sent you to talk me into taking the offer he made me, didn't he?"

She cackled at that. "I think Aaron knows better than to think I'll take *his* side on anything." She flipped the bacon and poured the slimy egg mixture into another frying pan, which she placed over a medium flame.

"So you don't think I should take the job?"

"Well, it *is* a lot of money to turn down. And being the head of the legal department for Sutherland Industries is a prestigious position for someone so young. But I didn't raise you with a silver spoon in your mouth...no matter how many times your father tried to shove one down your throat. I trust you to do what's right...for *you*."

He nodded, though she didn't see it.

Nash's parents had divorced when he was two years old, and being raised by a single mother in a modest home had kept him firmly grounded. Something his father knew nothing about. The man flashed his money and power every chance he got.

Nash walked over to the counter and poured himself a cup of coffee. "Good. Because I'm *not* taking the job."

"What job?" The timid voice came from behind them.

They turned to see Bailey standing in the doorway, wearing his white button-down shirt with the sleeves rolled up to her elbows. The hem grazed her mid-thigh, which brought only one question to mind. *What the hell was she wearing underneath?*

"Oh, I'm sorry. I didn't know you had company," his mother said, offering a quick smile. "I hope I didn't wake you, dear. I'm Nash's mother, Victoria."

Bailey offered her a shy smile. "I'm Bailey."

His mom glared at him. "You could have warned me you had a guest."

Nash walked over and settled his arm around Bailey's shoulders, grinning. "Bailey's not a guest, Mom. She's my wife."

The woman blinked and said, "That's not funny." Then she turned, slipped on an oven mitt, and pulled the hot biscuits from the oven.

He waited for her to put them down. "You're right, it's not. We got married at the courthouse yesterday. I was going to call you, but everything happened so fast that I didn't get a chance."

Not saying a word, his mom stirred the eggs continuously until they solidified. When he heard her sniffling, he cringed, walked up behind her, and placed a hand on her shoulder. "I'm sorry, Mom. Please don't be upset. I should have told you sooner. I didn't even think how you would feel about not being there."

Using a fork, she moved the bacon onto some paper towels to drain. Then she turned off the burners, stirred the cooked eggs once more, and set the spatula down so hard it clattered on the counter. "Why would I be upset? Because my only son gets married and doesn't invite me to his wedding? Of course I'm not upset," she said, her voice quivering.

Damn it. This wasn't the way he'd planned to share the news with her, but he was going to have to tell her the whole truth to keep her from being mad at him. "Mom, Bailey's pregnant."

Her head snapped to him and she stared hard, as if she were waiting on the punchline. When one didn't come, she turned her teary gaze onto Bailey. "Y-you're pregnant...with my son's child? I'm going to be a...grandmother?"

Bailey's cheeks reddened, and she bit her bottom lip nervously. "I'm sorry. I should probably leave you two alone so you can talk." She turned to leave.

"Oh, no. Please stay." His mom stepped over to Bailey and smiled. "I admit I'm a little surprised, especially since I didn't know my son was in a serious relationship. But this is...well, it's wonderful news!" She squealed in delight. "A grandma..." she repeated, as if the word was foreign to her.

Nash didn't bother correcting her about Bailey and him being in a relationship—much less a serious one—before they married. How she came to be his wife was nobody's business but theirs. Besides, the last thing he wanted to do was embarrass her any more than he probably had already when he'd stupidly blurted out she was pregnant without consulting her first.

God, I'm a fucking idiot.

But he'd suspected his mom would get over her irritation the moment she found out there was a grandbaby in her future. Thankfully, he was right. For the next several minutes, his mom chattered non-stop about all the things she planned to buy for their child. *The kid isn't even here yet and is already spoiled rotten.*

Nash grinned, though. His mother's excitement was not only contagious, but Bailey seemed to be relaxing more and enjoying the instant camaraderie she'd found with her new mother-in-law. Every time his wife smiled, she took his breath away. It was something he planned to make sure she did more often.

"Oh, my God!" his mom shrieked. "I just realized I'm intruding on your honeymoon." She reached for her purse on the counter. "I should go and leave you two lovebirds alone."

"It's okay," Bailey said, shaking her head. "We didn't have any plans today."

Ha! Speak for yourself. Nash had plenty of plans today and not a single damn one included them leaving the bedroom, much less hanging out with his mother. But he wasn't about to say that out loud and hurt her feelings.

Nash nodded to the stove. "What about breakfast? Aren't you going to stay and eat?"

"You two enjoy it." His mother started out the kitchen door, but stopped at the last minute. "Bailey, how about I take you to lunch next week? It would give us girls a chance to get to know each other better."

"Sure, I'd like that," Bailey replied, offering a sincere smile.

His mom wrapped her arms around Bailey and squeezed tight. "Welcome to the family." She released her, then glanced over to her son. "Oh, and, Nash…do me a favor. Call your father."

Yeah. That'll be a cold day in hell. Despite her request, though, he grinned. "I knew you had an ulterior motive for this visit."

She winked at him, then headed out the door.

Nash sank into one of the wooden chairs and blew out a breath. Well, that went better than he'd expected. Bailey walked over to the stove and picked up a small piece of bacon, popping it into her mouth. "You hungry? I can make you a plate."

Nash started to rise. "Here, let me—"

"No. You don't have to do everything for me. I'm pregnant, not an invalid. I'm quite capable of plating some food. Besides, if you don't let me do things for you, too, then this is never going to work."

He nodded and sat back down. "Okay. The dishes are in the second cabinet on your left."

When she reached up in the cabinet, Nash's first thought was he would have to lower the shelves to accommodate for her height. But when the back of her shirt rose several inches, showing off even more of those long, sexy legs he wanted to wrap around his waist, he changed his mind.

Damn shelves could stand to be taken up a notch or two.

Even after Bailey managed to get the plates down, Nash couldn't take his eyes off her. Especially when she dropped the dish towel on the floor and bent over to retrieve it. The white shirt she wore tightened across her ass and there was no panty line in sight.

Knowing he'd put her luggage in the guest room to keep her from tripping over it until they could unpack it, he'd bet everything he owned she wasn't wearing anything underneath. Just the thought alone sent an ache straight to his groin.

As if she'd read his thoughts, Bailey glanced over her shoulder and said, "By the way, I hope it's okay that I borrowed your shirt. My suitcases seem to be conveniently missing, and I wasn't going to put on my clothes from yesterday."

Heaven help me. The woman probably didn't even realize it, but she was killing him slowly. All he wanted to know was what the hell she had on beneath that fucking shirt. And it was about damn time he found out. "Bailey, come here, please."

"One second, I'm almost done."

"No, just leave it." His voice came out more curt than he meant it to.

She turned and gave him a puzzled look, but set the plate down and walked over to him without any hesitation. He shoved his chair back from the solid oak table and maneuvered her directly in front of him. "Sit," he ordered, gesturing to the table behind her.

Bailey perched on the edge as asked, but stared at him warily.

Nash didn't hesitate. He lowered his head and kissed her left thigh, slowly trailing his tongue over her soft skin. She froze at the unexpected touch, but the moment her body relaxed, he moved to the right thigh and gave it the same treatment. Then, placing both hands on her knees, he gently spread her legs apart.

His cock twitched beneath the seam of his jeans. *Fuck, yeah. No panties.*

He'd already figured she wasn't wearing any, but seeing her without them caused a much stronger reaction than just thinking it. Wordlessly, Nash reached out and stroked two fingers through her slick folds, coating each one with her wetness.

"Um, Nash…" She panted softly as he continued to fondle her. "Don't you want to eat first?"

His mouth watered at the scent of her arousal. "Sweetheart, you just read my mind."

126

CHAPTER NINETEEN

BAILEY STIFFENED. "HERE?"

"Oh, yeah. Right here, baby," Nash whispered, then slid his fingers inside her.

A strangled sound left her throat. *Oh God.*

He worked his fingers in and out slowly, then used his free hand to coax her into laying back on the hard table. The coolness of the wood seeped through the back of her shirt, but the cold farmhouse table was the least of her concerns. Her discomfort had way more to do with the way she was spread out before him like an all-you-can-eat buffet.

Not that he seemed to mind.

Nash—who was getting an intimate, up-close view of her goodies in broad daylight—licked his lips as if he couldn't decide what to sample first. Within seconds, he made his decision and went straight for the main course, suctioning his mouth directly over her clit.

Her back arched in ecstasy, and she clutched fistfuls of his hair. *Okay, so maybe here is not so bad, after all.*

His agile fingers and skilled tongue drew out every gasp she tried to swallow. Somehow, in their short time together, he'd figured out right where to touch her to set her off like a firing squad. The virile man had skills, and—holy hell—oral sex was at the top of that list.

The bold caress of his lips sent blood humming through her veins, and her eyes fluttered closed. A gripping sensation took hold of her body while the stirring of primal needs tampered with her sanity.

From the beginning, she'd tried to keep Nash at bay, but the persistent man had breached every defense she'd thrown at him. Didn't he realize the emotional roadblocks she'd put in his path were meant to protect both of them when all of this came to a screeching halt? Yet, he refused to avoid them. Instead, he continued to plow right through the sonsofbitches and kept on going.

Worst. Fucking. Driver. Ever.

Unfortunately, that made her the crash test dummy passenger, riding shotgun, without a seatbelt or airbag to protect her from the head-on collision she saw coming with the brick wall of heartache. There'd be nothing to cushion the blow, and she only hoped the baby wouldn't be collateral damage. *Damn it. Don't do it, Bailey. Don't fall for him.*

But sadly, it was too late. His strategy was working, and every moment she spent with him cracked her heart open a little wider. God. He was just too much to resist.

Bailey's body quivered as she absorbed the way his mouth felt on her. The lapping motions he made with his tongue quickened the aching tension coiling inside her and the breathless urgency took over. Desire pooled around her, while waves of pleasure crashed against her core. She moaned loudly, giving in to the sensations.

The moment her body convulsed, Nash tightened his grip on her thighs and fed on her like a starving man who'd just been given his first substantial meal in days. When her strangled cries quieted and her body went limp, he stood and swiftly lifted her into his strong arms.

"What are you doing?"

"Taking my wife to bed," he answered simply, then headed down the hall.

After laying her gently on her pillow, he stripped off his unbuttoned jeans and tossed them aside. Bailey's gaze lowered to his solid erection, and she licked her lips.

"See something you like?" His husky voice vibrated in the air.

Her eyes lifted to his and her cheeks warmed. The sexy bastard had read her mind and wore a smug grin. "Maybe," she teased, adding a nonchalant shrug to punctuate her answer. Then she smiled at him.

His brow rose and his eyes lit with challenge. "Just maybe, huh?"

Teasing a man in bed was a new experience for her, but one she liked very much. And judging from his reaction, she wasn't the only one enjoying it.

The moment he lunged for her, Bailey rolled away and scrambled across the bed, giggling. Grabbing her by the ankle, he flipped her over and hauled her back to him, wedging his muscled thighs between her legs. His hard length rubbed against her as he leaned down to her ear and growled, "I think I should do something about that maybe of yours."

"You should," she agreed, repositioning her hips to better accept him.

He inched his thick, swollen head inside her, and a moan gurgled in her throat. She waited for him to take her, to push deeper, so she could feel that delicious intrusion that always took her breath away as her flesh gave way to his. But instead, he stilled himself above her, bracketing his arms around her head to hold himself up.

"Tell me what you want, baby."

What? No. She didn't feel like talking right now. Her body burned for him to move inside her, to claim her, to fuck her until she couldn't see straight. That's what she wanted. Screw talking about it.

Frustrated by his hesitation, Bailey lifted her pelvis to grind against him. But he shifted and withdrew even more. "Uh-uh. If you want it, you're going to damn well say it first. Now tell me."

The intensity of his blue eyes and the slight smile tugging at the corner of his mouth told her this was no longer a game. At least not one she would win.

Well, fuck.

"I want it."

He grinned sinfully. "Want what?"

"You. Or more specifically, your dick—"

She gasped.

Without hesitation, Nash had thrust his hips forward and sank fully into her depths. Overwhelmed by the unexpected invasion, her inner muscles clamped down hard on him, bonding them together.

He groaned and blew out a slow breath. "God, you have no clue how good this feels. You're so fucking tight."

He was wrong about that. She knew exactly how good it felt. How good *he* felt. The heavy weight of him pressing her into the mattress as he buried himself in her. The muscled hardness of his body straining against hers. The way his fingers dug into her shoulders, as if he needed something tangible to hold onto.

Yeah, she knew.

But it was nothing compared to how she felt when he began rolling his hips and sending shock waves of pleasure rippling through her. Her thighs quivered each time he pumped his magnificent cock inside her, probing her slick heat with a slow, repetitive pattern. His smoldering eyes held hers with intent.

Bailey remembered that look.

He was waiting for her to unravel beneath him, so he could watch her dive over the edge of insanity into the fires of orgasmic bliss. But, this time, she was taking him with her. Sinewy arms caged her in, but she'd be damned if she was just going to lie there and let him take possession of her without giving him something in return.

If I burn, we both burn.

Bailey raked her nails across his ribs, and he shuddered. Yearning to taste him, she leaned up and brushed her tongue along his bottom lip, then sucked it into her mouth and gave it a quick nip. His speed increased, and he grew thicker and harder inside her. Stripping away the last of her restraint, she pulled back and quickly unbuttoned her shirt, slid it aside, and bared her breasts.

That one little move apparently unshackled the primal need growing between them. He mumbled something incoherent under his breath, closed his lips firmly around one pebbled nub, and they fell off the cliff...together.

Nash stroked into her several more times, each thrust slower than the last, until he stopped altogether and held himself deep inside her, pulsing and throbbing. His eyes slid shut in ecstasy as he threw his head back, his grunts of completion muffled by her cries of release. Then he lowered his head to her neck and breathed heavily.

Several quiet minutes passed before Nash shifted beside her and pulled her into his strong arms. "You okay?" he asked, concern tightening his voice.

She sighed contently and snuggled into his chest. "Mmm-hmm."

He kissed the top of her head.

After a few moments of silence, Bailey said, "I, um…liked your mom."

Nash chuckled. "Good. Because she's going to spoil our child rotten. She's been asking me for grandbabies since I graduated law school. She always said she didn't want to be an old lady by the time I gave her one."

Bailey glanced up at him and folded her hand under her chin, smiling. "Will I like your dad, too?"

His brows furrowed and his body tensed. "No. Probably not."

Puzzled, she waited for him to elaborate, but he didn't. "Is there any particular reason why?"

"Because I don't even like him half the time."

"Oh. Is that why you won't take his job offer?"

"Yes. He's an overbearing, pompous ass. I have no doubt he would be checking up on me and questioning every decision I made. It's not worth it. He's always tried to control me and has been pulling this kind of shit for years. The last time I spoke to him, I told him to take his job and shove it up his ass. That was three months ago."

"Maybe if you talked to him about how you feel…"

"You don't think I've tried in the past?" He plunged his fingers through his hair. "Aaron Sutherland doesn't hear anything that isn't coming out of his own mouth. I don't want anything to do with him or the family business."

"But y-you're his son."

"So?"

"So don't you want a relationship with your dad?"

Nash barked out a sarcastic laugh. "I had a relationship with him. A shitty one. So I got out while I could."

"If he's trying to make amends through your mom, though…"

"He's not. The only thing my dad is trying to do is get me to take that fucking position at Sutherland Industries. It's not going to happen." Nash slid out from under her and swung his legs off the bed. "I'll never ask that man for anything as long as I live."

She placed one hand on his bicep. "Nash…."

He glanced over his shoulder at her.

"I know you're upset with him, but I… Well, I lost my mom in a car accident when I was five years old." She blinked back the tears forming in her eyes and swallowed hard.

Nash turned to her, cradling her cheek with his hand. "I'm so sorry, sweetheart. I didn't know."

She shook her head, pushing away the sorrow welling up inside her. "It's okay. It was a long time ago. But I can't call her, talk to her, or even argue with her anymore. So although I know you're mad now, don't write your father off completely over something as silly as a job offer. There may come a day when you can't talk to him and you'll wish you could."

He sighed. "I'll think about it, okay?"

She smiled at him. "That's all I ask. Besides, our baby will probably want to meet his or her grandfather one day."

"Oh, this kid is in for a real treat, then," he said, rolling his eyes. He leaned over and kissed her on the mouth. "Speaking of which, I'm sure you're starving. Why don't I grab our food before it gets any colder and we'll have breakfast in bed? Then we can take a shower…together." He waggled his brows suggestively.

She grinned at him, fully aware of what that shower would lead to, but nodded anyway. Everything Bailey had ever wanted in a husband was right there in front of her. Loving. Playful. Kind. Irresistible. All she had to do was hang on to it, to *him*, and keep from screwing it all up.

Sure, in the beginning she'd bet against them working as a couple, but what she hadn't known at the time was just how right things could be. Nash had stacked the deck in their favor, and although she'd never been much of a gambler…

Well, she was all in.

CHAPTER TWENTY

$\sim\!\!\sim\!\!\bullet\!\!\sim\!\!\sim$

THE FOLLOWING WEEK, Nash left his office two hours early. It wasn't something he did very often, but his favorite part of having his own practice was having control over his own schedule, which was something he couldn't do in the corporate world. He always knew he would settle down eventually and didn't want to be an absentee husband or an occasional father.

He made a quick stop at the florist to pick up a dozen long-stemmed red roses, and then headed home to surprise Bailey. When he arrived, though, she wasn't there to greet him as she usually did when she heard him coming down the driveway.

But he was early. Maybe she was in the shower. Or taking a nap.

He placed the aromatic bouquet and his black briefcase on the kitchen counter and headed toward the bedroom to check on her. But as he rounded the corner and stepped into the hallway, he stopped in his tracks. A pair of black satin panties lay smack dab in the middle of the floor in front of him.

At first, he was puzzled, but then he grinned.

Obviously, his adorable wife must've called the office after he'd left for the day and the secretary had told Bailey he was on his way home. The more time he spent with Bailey, the more she teased him—in and out of the bedroom—but this was taking things to a whole new level. *The little vixen.*

Nash swiped the panties from the floor and ran his fingers over the silky texture, letting the sensation torment his libido. His cock hardened and he reached down to adjust the uncomfortable swelling. When that didn't help, he popped open the button on his pants, slid down his zipper, and freed his raging hard-on from the constraints of clothing.

Ah, much better.

He continued to the bedroom, loosening his tie and unbuttoning his shirt as he went, but paused at the bedroom door. Soft grunting sounds came from the other side, and they were getting louder.

No fucking way. She's…masturbating?

He envisioned her lying in their bed, legs spread, while running her small hand down her slim body until she reached that sensitive bundle of nerves he loved to nibble on so much. No doubt she'd be circling it in slow motion, building the tension, until her body exploded beneath her own touch.

Then he heard her mutter, "Oh, yeah, that's the spot."

Nash steadied himself against the door. *Motherfucker.*

He wasn't sure if he was pissed she hadn't waited for him or turned on that she was apparently about to make herself come. But then his dick twitched and grew even harder, giving him his answer.

Nash groaned quietly, and his stomach tightened. He was half-tempted to listen to her finish herself off, but… *Like hell.* He wanted to join that party, wanted to see that wild, glazed look in her eyes, wanted to hear her panting his name as he delivered the pleasure she sought.

But as he twisted the knob, a man's rough voice muttered, "You like it right there?"

Nash paused. There was another man in his bedroom…with *his* fucking wife!

Fire shot through his veins, and he barreled through the door to find a young guy in overalls standing on one side of the bed, leaning against the wall, while a fully clothed Bailey stood on the opposite side.

She squeaked and her hand flew to her chest. "Jesus, you scared me!" Then her eyes lowered and she covered her mouth and giggled. "Oh, my God. What are you doing?"

Nash glanced down, realizing his dick was still hanging out of his pants and he was holding Bailey's panties in his hand. *Sonofabitch.* He twisted away from the man, shoved his junk back inside, zipped up his pants, then shoved the panties into his pocket before turning back to face them. "What the fuck is going on here?" he growled.

At his tone, Bailey's brow rose suspiciously. "What is it you *think* is going on?"

"I'm not in the mood to play guessing games. Just answer the damn question."

Her gaze narrowed and she pursed her lips. "No."

"No?" Nash clenched his teeth and his hands fisted at his sides. "What the hell do you mean *no*?"

"You heard me. I don't know what has you in such a snit, but until you apologize for speaking to me like that, I'm not answering jack shit." She crossed her arms.

The man in the overalls raised both hands in surrender and shook his head. "Hey, man, I'm just here delivering a dresser. I didn't do anything, I swear."

Nash glanced past him at the new dresser against the wall. "Where's your delivery truck? I didn't see one outside."

"The lady had me park it around back so I could bring the dresser through the kitchen. She said it would be easier. We'd just gotten it into place when you came in."

"*We?*" Nash asked, turning a sharp eye onto his wife, who only stuck out her stubborn chin more.

"Well, yeah. Your wife—"

"Is pregnant," Nash said, rudely cutting him off.

The man's eyes widened. "Well, it's not mine."

"No shit, it's mine. Now get the fuck out of my house."

"Nash!" Bailey exclaimed as the delivery man hightailed it out the door as fast as he could. The moment they heard the front door swing closed, she glared at him in disgust. "What the hell has come over you?"

"Me? What's wrong with you? You shouldn't be moving heavy furniture in your condition."

"Oh God. Stop being so dramatic. I didn't even lift the stupid dresser. I just helped him scoot it across the floor."

"I don't care. You should have waited for me. I would have moved it for you."

"Well, I didn't. Sue me for trying to get it done before you got home." She motioned to the bed, where her two large suitcases lay side by side. "I wanted to unpack now so I could spend the rest of the evening with *you*." She turned away from him and huffed out a breath.

Shit. He'd left work early because he'd wanted the same thing—to spend time with her. But he'd screwed everything up. Feeling like an idiot, he walked up behind her and touched her shoulder. "Bailey, I'm sorry."

She pulled away. "For what exactly? Yelling at me or thinking I was screwing around on you?"

"I didn't think you were—" She cast a challenging glance over her shoulder at him. "Okay, fine. Damn it, I heard you grunting and groaning, then heard a man's voice. What the hell did you expect me to think?"

"You should have trusted me."

Her hurt tone punched him in the gut, and he cringed. "I know."

"You also shouldn't have spoken to either of us that way. That poor man didn't deserve it, and I sure as hell didn't."

"I know that too." Testing her receptiveness, he reached out once more and ran his finger along her arm. This time, she didn't retreat from his touch. "I'm a jackass. Will you forgive me?"

"Maybe," she said, half-smiling. "But I need to know one thing first."

"What's that?"

She looked at him dead-on, her face serious. "Why did you run in here with your dick hanging out of your pants? Were you trying to intimidate him?"

Nash laughed, then ran a hand through his hair. "I found your panties laying on the floor in the hallway. I thought maybe you were trying to tell me something."

Bailey giggled. "They must have fallen out of my suitcases when I carried them in here."

"You picked them up yourself?" He wanted to beat his head against a wall. "Damn it, Bailey. Those are fucking heavy. Do I have to tie you to the bed when I leave for work so you don't overexert yourself?"

Glancing down at the large bulge in his pants, she said, "I have a feeling that if you tied me to a bed, it wouldn't keep me from overexerting myself. Probably would only make it worse."

"Oh, yeah?" Nash leaned in and nuzzled her ear. "I made dinner reservations for us tonight. Why don't we go out to eat and then come home and find out?"

"You're on, but I need a quick shower first before we go."

"That's okay. We've got two hours before we have to leave. Plenty of time for you to get ready."

She flipped open the suitcase closest to her, grabbed some clothes, and then headed for the bathroom. A moment later, he heard the shower door open and the water turned on. He considered joining her, but knew they'd never make it to dinner on time if he did. So Nash settled on the edge of the bed to wait for her.

"You know, if you would have just let me help you unpack these when you first moved in, you wouldn't have had to carry them in here."

"I told you I would just wait until the new dresser arrived. I didn't want you to have to move your clothes to make room for mine. It was just temporary. Didn't kill me."

No, but he might if he caught her lugging around anything that heavy again while she was pregnant.

As he sat there, something in her open luggage caught his attention. A newspaper, neatly folded in half, stuck out from beneath her clothes with the word "Sutherland" in bold black ink. Nash slid the paper out and opened it.

To his surprise, it was the article that had started the entire argument between him and his father. Aaron Sutherland had given an interview to a reporter where he'd named Nash as the new head of the legal department for Sutherland Industries…before his father had even asked him if he'd wanted the damn position.

And he didn't. Not in the least.

His father knew he would turn down the position. Taking that job would have come with too steep of a price. But where his tyrant father was concerned, business always came before family, and this had been his way of trying to force Nash into the position. Or what his dad referred to as "taking his rightful place in the family business."

But Nash had never wanted to be like his father. He didn't aspire to have some fancy corporate job in Houston. In law school, he'd dreamed of opening his own practice in a smaller town, one where he could get to know his clients on a personal level and help those individuals solve their legal problems, ethically and without a large financial burden. That was much more gratifying than protecting a corporation's assets.

Because he'd never wanted to ask his dad for anything, Nash had used the inheritance he'd received from his grandparents at age twenty-one to pay for law school, purchase his home, and open his business in Flat Rock, Texas. Nash made a decent living. He wasn't rich by any means, but...well, he couldn't give a shit less.

The moment he'd seen the article, he had marched straight into his dad's office, tossed the newspaper on his old man's desk, and very clearly told him to go fuck himself. Because he'd had enough of Aaron Sutherland trying to control him.

But why did Bailey have a copy of it? She hadn't even known Nash back when the article came out, much less his father.

He wanted to ask her about it, but he couldn't bring himself to do it. Not after the stunt he'd just pulled. The hurt in her voice when she'd told him he should have trusted her had damn near killed him. The last thing he wanted was the mother of his unborn child to think he didn't believe in her. Even if she did have a track record of keeping things from him.

But that was all in the past, wasn't it?

They were married now. Husband and wife. And they were growing closer and closer with each passing day. Their first week had been busy, consisting of furniture shopping, picking out their baby's first outfit, and arguing at the car dealership for an hour before she finally relented and let him buy her a new car to replace her old one he'd sold.

And just yesterday, Bailey had gone to lunch with his mother and couldn't wait to get home to tease him about the half-naked childhood photos his mom had shared with her. Then he'd made them popcorn and held her hand on the couch while they'd watched a movie together. Things were great between them. So there was no way he was going to screw it all up by making her feel like he was giving her the third degree.

He'd asked for her trust and she'd given it, opening up to him more and more each day. Nash wasn't willing to jeopardize that over some stupid newspaper article.

"Nash, I'm almost done, but I forgot to grab a towel," Bailey hollered over the sound of the rushing water. "Would you mind getting me one?"

"Sure, no problem." He slid the newspaper back into her suitcase just how he found it and headed to the bathroom.

The mirror had already fogged over and the scent of her coconut shampoo infused with the rising steam. Bailey stood in the shower, just beyond the frosted glass door, running soapy hands over her breasts as the water trickled down to the notch between her slender thighs.

Desire shot through him, hard and fast, and presented itself in the form of a rapidly growing cock. One he very much wanted to fuck his gorgeous wife with. So instead of fetching her a towel, he quickly stripped off his clothes and stepped into the shower behind her.

Surprised, Bailey turned to face him, glancing down at his swollen member. "What are you doing?"

"Looks like we're going to be late for dinner."

CHAPTER TWENTY-ONE

Two weeks.

That was how long Bailey had been married to the man of her dreams. Not only did he treat her like a queen, but he made it his mission in life to satisfy her every need—in and out of the bedroom. She couldn't imagine a more perfect husband than Nash Sutherland. And thankfully, he was all hers.

So what if their relationship had developed a little differently than a normal couple's? The undeniable connection they shared had bonded them in every sense of the word, and it was the best feeling in the world.

Bailey snuggled deeper into his chest as Nash's fingers roamed up and down her bare back, evoking pleasant sensations of tenderness and affection. A sigh of contentment escaped her lips.

"Can I ask you something?" he asked softly, sounding unsure of himself.

After a curious glance to his expressionless face, she nodded.

"What happened between you and Doug? I mean, I know you said you caught him cheating on your wedding day, but..."

Bailey hesitated, but with Nash being her husband, he had a right to hear the whole story. "I married him, which was stupid, since I knew something wasn't right between us. Against my better judgment, I went through with it, anyway. After we said our I dos, the entire wedding party moved to the adjoining reception hall where the guests waited for us. I didn't know almost anyone there, except for a few of my coworkers. The rest were Doug's family and friends." She looked up at Nash to see if he was paying attention and found him staring at her, hanging on her every word.

"Go on," he encouraged.

"Doug's pretentious mother had insisted I wear one of those poofy, Cinderella-type dresses, but I knew I would get hot after a few dances. So I compromised by bringing another gown with me. Thank God I did. About an hour into the reception, I practically had a heat stroke and went to the dressing room to change into the other dress I'd brought, which was much shorter and cooler. It was the one I was wearing the night I met you."

"Man, I loved that dress. You looked sexy as hell in it, but I couldn't wait to take it off you." Nash leaned down, brushed his lips against hers, and then smiled. "God. It makes me horny just thinking about it."

"That's exactly the reaction I'd hoped Doug would have when he saw me in it."

Nash's eyes narrowed, and a muscle ticked in his jaw. "Okay, fast forward through things like that or I'm going to go find Doug and kick the shit out of him."

"Okay, okay," she said, giggling at his jealous streak. "So by the time I got back to the reception, Doug was missing in action. Apparently, he'd told his mother he wanted to make a toast to our guests, so she handed me a microphone and asked me to find him. He'd been knocking back glasses of champagne, one after another, so I think she worried he'd make an ass out of himself."

"And he still managed to do that."

She shook her head furiously. "No. Actually, I did that for him."

His brow quirked. "What do you mean?"

"I found him in the kitchen. His pants were around his ankles, and he was balls deep in his secretary. Neither of them had heard me come in over all the dirty things he was spewing to her. I was in shock, of course. So I did the only thing I could think of. I turned on the microphone. When they still didn't notice me, I hit the button on the automatic partition window, which separated the kitchen from the reception hall. As the partition lifted, all the guests witnessed what Doug was doing, including his mother. Before he could get his pants up, I slapped him and walked out."

Nash shook his head in disgust. "Your ex-husband is a stupid sonofabitch."

"Tell me about it."

"So how did you end up at Rowdy's?"

"I stormed out of the reception before realizing I didn't have my cell phone or my car, and I wasn't about to go back inside to ask someone for a ride. Besides, all of my things were already moved into Doug's house and I wasn't going to go back there. I had nowhere else to go. I just needed to think, to figure out what I was going to do, so I started walking and ended up at the bar."

"So why didn't you just get the marriage annulled? It would have been cheaper and quicker than a divorce."

"I'd planned on it, but then…I met you." Guilt sloshed around in her stomach and a frown tugged at her mouth. "After what we—I mean, what *I* did…well, I just figured I wasn't any better than Doug. Even if the marriage meant nothing to him, I was legally his wife. What I did with you was wro—"

"Don't." There was no mistaking the warning in his tone, but Nash wrapped his hand gently around her neck and tilted her face up to his. His eyes held only tenderness. "Sweetheart, don't ever say what we did that night was wrong. It wasn't. It was fate, stepping in to make things right for you, for us. All of us. We conceived our child that night."

Bailey closed her eyes and rested her forehead against his warm lips. "I know. I didn't mean it like that. It's just…" Her words cut off and she sighed heavily.

"You didn't want to be a hypocrite?"

She cringed, but nodded. "Yes."

"Do you still love him?"

"No, that's the thing. I never loved Doug."

Nash's mouth fell open. "But that day at your apartment, I asked you if you loved your husband. You said you did."

"I lied. I needed time to figure things out for myself, but you kept pushing. I had to tell you something to get you to give me some breathing room. Besides, I only thought I loved Doug. I wanted the security of marriage and thought that once we were intimate, my feelings would deepen. But anything I felt for him flew out the window the minute I stepped into that kitchen. I never even shed a tear over him. I was pissed about what he had done, but I wasn't heartbroken over losing him. Before I'd made it to the bar, I'd already realized how un-in-love with Doug I truly was."

"Are you sure?"

"What? You don't believe me?"

"It's not that. It's just…you were a virgin when I met you. You must have thought a lot of the guy if you were saving yourself for your wedding night."

"Hardly. I wasn't doing that for *him*. I know this is probably going to sound silly, but I…I wanted my mother to be proud of me. She was the reason why I waited. It had nothing to do with Doug."

"Then why did you sleep with me? What changed your mind? I didn't push you into doing something you didn't want, did I?"

"No, not at all. You were wonderful to me." She smiled at him. "I had never had a guy treat me the way you did that night. I felt a strong connection to you, and I knew that was what I'd been waiting on all along. I needed you to touch me."

"You have no clue how much I wanted you that night. But, I swear, all you had to do was tell me no, and I would have kept my hands to myself." He kissed her forehead.

"Nash, I don't doubt that for a second. I also don't regret anything that happened—between us or walking in on Doug while he was screwing around on me. Even if I could go back in time and change it all, I wouldn't. I just want to keep moving forward…with *you*."

She felt him smile. "Good. Because that's what I want too."

A surge of endorphins flooded her system. Was that his way of telling her he was falling for her? God, she hoped so. Because she didn't want to be the only one having those kinds of feelings. The last thing she wanted was to be in another one-sided relationship that turned sour.

His free hand moved down to her stomach and rubbed lightly.

"I'm thinking I'm going to have to get your hand surgically removed if you keep doing that."

Nash laughed. "Tough shit. Get used to it."

"I already am," she said, smiling up at him. She loved when he touched her belly.

"You haven't been getting nauseated lately. Maybe the morning sickness is already subsiding."

"But I'll miss it so much," she said, sarcasm tickling her voice.

"Well, I've been reading those baby books I bought for us. You could still end up with heartburn and indigestion. That's something to look forward to."

"Oh, and don't forget my personal favorite: hemorrhoids."

Nash chuckled and nuzzled into her neck. "Mmm. That's sexy as hell."

She laughed and pushed him away. "I'm probably going to be so big that getting up is going to be a chore."

He winked suggestively. "Not for me, it won't be."

"I hope you're attracted to sumo wrestlers, then," she said with a teasing smile. "Because I'm pretty sure I'm going to resemble one."

"Only if you're having twins. They do run on my mom's side of the family, you know."

Bailey blinked. *What? Oh, fuck that.* His mother hadn't said a word about it during their lunch date. "I'd kill you first," she threatened, gigging him in the ribs.

"Ouch!" he said, rubbing his side. "That isn't fair. I can't do that to you."

"Well, this is all your fault, anyway. If you'd have just left me alone in the bar that night..." She grinned playfully.

Nash grabbed her and pulled her on top of him, his member hardening fast between her legs. "Then we wouldn't be lying naked in this bed right now."

"True," she said, angling her body until his hard length slid inside her. Placing her hands on his chest, she began moving. "But if our baby suddenly becomes two babies, I'm going to strangle you."

CHAPTER TWENTY-TWO

NASH SAT AT his desk, studying a case file for one of his clients
while whistling an upbeat tune. He glanced at the clock. A few
more hours to go before he would head home, but he couldn't wait
for his workday to end. Tonight was the night. He was finally going
to tell Bailey exactly how he felt about her.

They'd only been married three short weeks, but he couldn't
even remember his life before her. It was such a distant memory.
Like his brain and heart had highlighted only the moments she'd
participated in and tossed the rest aside. That was fine by him,
though. Because nothing mattered if his wife wasn't by his side.

His secretary knocked lightly on the door but didn't wait for
him to respond before entering the room. "Sorry, I know you're
busy. I just need to grab a file. One of your new clients is here to
pay his retainer fee. Also, this fax just came in for you."

He glanced at it, then set it down. "Thanks, Debbie. Any
messages?"

She bit her lip. "Well, um, your father called...again."

"Did he say what he wanted?"

"Same as always. He wants to talk to you, but he won't leave
a message or tell me what it's concerning." She moved to the large
wooden file cabinet along the far wall and opened the middle
drawer, searching through the alphabetized names for the file she
needed.

Nash sighed. *Why can't that damn man just give up already?* "It's
okay. I know what my dad wants to talk to me about. And I'm not
interested."

His dad was still trying to force him into having a conversation
he didn't want to have. Been there, done that. And it got him

nowhere. His persistent—and equally annoying—father just wouldn't accept that Nash didn't want the fucking job, all because the unreasonable old man didn't like to be told no.

Well, too fucking bad.

If he gave in and called him now, his father would only look at it as a victory. Nash wouldn't give him the satisfaction. In fact, he didn't give a shit if his law practice went belly up. He *wasn't* calling his father for anything. Ever.

"If my dad calls back again, tell him I'm in a meeting and won't be out of it until hell freezes over."

Debbie glanced over her shoulder and grinned. "Will do, Boss."

Sure, he'd promised Bailey he'd think about returning his call, but she didn't know his dad or how frustrating the asshole could be. If she did, she'd know the man wouldn't stop at anything to get what he wanted.

Immediately, his mind rewound to the week before when he'd found the newspaper article about his dad in Bailey's suitcase. He'd meant to ask her why she had it, but he'd forgotten all about—

"By the way, I want to know your wife's secret," Debbie said, breaking Nash's train of thought.

His mouth went dry. "Uh, secret?"

"Well, yeah. I mean, the woman obviously knows how to put you in a good mood. You've been smiling nonstop for weeks, and I've heard you in here whistling all morning long. I'm assuming Mrs. Sutherland has something to do with it. I've never seen you so happy."

Nash smiled at that. It was true. He *was* happy. "I love her."

The moment he said the words out loud, his heart thumped inside his chest. God, that felt good. He couldn't wait to say it again, but this time, to Bailey herself.

"Never a doubt in my mind," Debbie said, pulling the file she was looking for from the cabinet. Then she headed out the door.

Nash went back to work, hoping to finish up what he was working on before the end of the day. No way in hell was he taking his work home with him. He had plans and they didn't involve sitting at his desk while going over his next court hearing.

A half hour passed before Debbie opened his door again. "Nash, there's an urgent call for you on line two."

He groaned. "It's not my father, is it?"

"No, it's your wife."

His hand flew to the phone, knocking it off the cradle, before he picked it up and lifted it to his ear, punching the button for line two. "Bailey, what's wrong?"

"I need you to come home." Her strained voice sounded weak.

"What is it? What's going on?"

She hesitated, then whispered, "I…I started bleeding."

His stomach sank and a knot formed in his throat, but somehow he managed to reply in a calm voice. "I'll be there in less than ten minutes."

"Okay," she replied, then sniffled.

"Baby, it's okay. Everything's going to be just fine." He closed his eyes, hoping like hell he was right about that. "I'm walking out the door right now."

They hung up and Nash reached for his suit jacket from the back of his chair. "Debbie, I need you to cancel the consultation appointment I had for this afternoon. There's an emergency at home."

"All right," Debbie replied. "Is your wife okay?"

Nash stared directly at her as the realization hit him. "No. She's not."

Then he ran out the office door, sprinted across the parking lot to his truck, and sped home as quickly as he could.

When he arrived, Bailey met him at the door, dry tear streaks marring her somber face. "I'm sorry I called. I didn't know what else—"

"No. Don't be. I want you to call me when something's wrong." Nash glanced back to the truck. "I called Doctor Stevenson on the way here. He's on duty at the hospital today, so they're going to page him the moment we arrive. Should I carry you to the truck?"

She shook her head, but allowed him to guide her. "Is that the doctor I was supposed to see next week for my first prenatal appointment?"

"Yes. He'll take good care of you, too." Nash opened the cab door and lifted her into the passenger seat. "Not only did he deliver me, but he's my dad's old poker buddy. He's been treating my family for years." He shut the door, ran around to the driver's side, and climbed behind the wheel.

As he started to pull away, Bailey placed her hand on his arm, gaining his attention. "Nash, I'm scared."

"Me, too, baby."

The twenty-minute drive to the hospital on the outskirts of Houston was the longest trip of his life. Nash ran every yellow light and even some red ones to get Bailey there as quickly as possible. The moment they arrived, he helped her inside and had her sit in a chair while he talked to the receptionist about paging the doctor. Almost immediately, a nurse called them back to triage and took Bailey's vitals. Everything seemed normal, which was a good sign as far as he was concerned.

Moments later, the nurse led them to a large room and asked Bailey to change into a gown. She was lying back on a gurney with a small pale green sheet covering her when the doctor entered the room, wheeling in a machine. He clasped his hand on Nash's back in a friendly gesture and then introduced himself to Bailey, shaking her hand.

She looked pale and fragile, like she would start sobbing at any moment. Nash couldn't stand it. He knew she was assuming the worst…that she was having a miscarriage. *Sonofabitch.* Just the idea alone sickened him.

Doctor Stevenson explained that he was going to perform a vaginal sonogram on her to get a look at the baby and make sure everything was all right. As he started the procedure, Nash moved to Bailey's side and reached for her hand. Her cold fingers trembled beneath his, so he wrapped his hand around hers to warm it and held on tight.

His heart lodged in his throat as he scrutinized the doctor's face for any signs of bad news. Unfortunately, the man was a professional and kept careful control over his expressions. His face revealed nothing. No wonder Nash's father always bitched about losing a bundle of money after their poker games.

When the doctor finished, he examined Bailey, then pulled off his gloves and tossed them in the trash. "Why don't Nash and I step out and let you get dressed, then we'll talk?"

Bailey stared at him, but didn't respond. She looked numb to everything and everyone around her. Nash was just about to argue that he wasn't leaving her side when Doctor Stevenson gave him an imperceptible nod toward the door. He wanted to talk to Nash…alone? *Shit. That can't be good.*

His wife seemed oblivious to the doctor's request, but Nash didn't want to worry her any more than necessary. At least not until he knew what they were up against. So he kissed her temple and squeezed her hand to reassure her. "I'll be right outside if you need me." Then he followed the doctor out the door.

The moment Nash stepped into the hallway and pulled the door shut behind him, he scrubbed his hand through his hair. "How bad is it, Doc?"

Stevenson shook his head and frowned. "We'll get to that in just a second. First, I need to ask you an important question. How well do you know your wife?"

Nash took a step back. "What kind of goddamn question is that?"

"A logical one. Last month you had me test you for sexually transmitted diseases, though you told me you weren't involved with anyone. Then three weeks ago, I run into your father on the golf course who tells me you got married. Now you're in here with a woman who claims to be carrying your child. None of it makes any sense."

My father knows about Bailey? Fuck. Of course, he does. His dad had always kept tabs on him. Why would this time be any different? "Look, it's complicated, okay? She's my wife now and I…well, I know her well enough."

"You sure about that?" Dr. Stevenson raised one brow. "Because I've done several DNA tests on babies whose mothers claimed had been fathered by a Sutherland, and not a single one of those claims proved to be true."

Nash didn't know what any of this had to do with Bailey, but he wasn't going to stand there and defend his reasons for marrying her. Screw dancing around the subject. Something was obviously wrong, and although he dreaded hearing what it was, he needed to. "None of this matters. I just need you to tell me if the baby is all right."

The doctor sighed and placed a hand on Nash's shoulder. "I'm sorry to tell you this, but there is no baby."

CHAPTER TWENTY-THREE

BAILEY SAT ALONE in the sterile-smelling room, taking deep breaths to keep the panic at bay. She knew something had happened. Something bad. Why else would the doctor ask Nash to step out of the room while she got dressed?

The door opened and Dr. Stevenson entered the room, followed by her husband. His glum face reeked of bad news as he slumped into the nearest chair and stared at the floor. He wouldn't even look at her.

But she didn't even have to ask. The doctor placed his cold hand on hers and his eyes softened, as he prepared to give her the horrible news. "Mrs. Sutherland, I'm afraid I have something to tell you that may be difficult to hear."

Bailey's breath caught in her throat. Every nerve ending stood on high alert. *No, no, no! This isn't happening!*

Grief fisted her heart in the palm of its hand, while sadness swept through her blood stream in a fast flowing current of sorrow. Using her free hand, she rubbed at the deep ache growing inside her chest. "I…I lost the baby, didn't I?" Her voice cracked and her eyes brimmed with tears.

"No."

No? She should have been relieved, but the way the doctor continued to stare at her sympathetically worried her even more. "Then what? What's wrong with our baby?"

"That's just it, Mrs. Sutherland. There is no baby. You *aren't* pregnant."

She shook her head furiously. "What are you talking about? Of course I'm pregnant."

"The bleeding you're experiencing is due to your monthly cycle. There is no pregnancy, and as far as I can tell, there never was. At least not recently."

Closing her eyes, Bailey rubbed at her temples. "What? That's not...possible. It doesn't make any sense. I *was* pregnant." She pointed at Nash. "Ask him. He was with me when I got the results. And this wasn't some home pregnancy test I did. I went to a doctor who confirmed it through bloodwork."

"Yes, Nash told me. But that doctor's clinic is currently being investigated for three counts of malpractice, I'm afraid. All of which were due to faulty test results."

What? No. This had to be some kind of sick joke. Her heart hammered against her ribcage. "B-but I missed my last period....and I even had morning sickness."

"Since you weren't my patient, and I didn't see you at the time, I can't say for certain what caused the symptoms. My best guess is that you may have had some sort of viral stomach bug or possibly food poisoning. Nash told me you were also going through a divorce at the time. Stress can lower your immunity and that, especially combined with an illness, has been known to cause women to miss a cycle."

Unable to believe any of it, she shook her head again. "No, it's just...not possible."

"Mrs. Sutherland, if you want, I can run more tests and check your bloodwork again, but I'm certain I'm not going to find anything that will change the outcome. You aren't pregnant."

"No, I..." Lightheaded, she swayed in place as a wide range of emotions swam through her. Confusion at how this could happen. Sadness over a child who had apparently never existed. Anger at the idiot doctor who led them to believe a baby was in their immediate future.

And then something else took hold. A debilitating fear rooted itself deep in her belly, shaking her from the inside out.

Nash.

He'd only married her because they'd thought she was carrying his child. Now that he knew she wasn't, would he want a divorce? No. Surely, he wasn't thinking that. He hadn't said a word—or even looked at her—since they'd returned to the room, but he had to be as shocked as she was and still processing it all.

Elbows on his thighs, Nash continued to stare at the tile floor with his fingers clasped tightly together between his legs. The anguish over losing a fictional child showed plainly on his grim face, casting a dark shadow.

In just a few short weeks, they'd experienced the same joys most expecting parents were gifted. The delight in picking out their baby's first gender-neutral outfit. The surprise in announcing the news to the grandmother-to-be. The pride of talking about their child's future hopes and dreams. Maybe to the doctor, the pregnancy had never existed, but to the two of them, the baby had been real…even if only in their hearts.

This isn't right. It isn't supposed to be like this. A stray tear dripped onto her cheek, and her body vibrated with the rage of injustice. "I just…want to go home."

Dr. Stevenson nodded. "I'll send the nurse in with your discharge papers."

Once he left, thick tension and cold silence filled the room.

She would have given anything for Nash to put his arms around her and tell her everything between them would be okay. To lift his gaze and give her the connection she needed now more than ever. But he didn't.

Instead, he sat back and crossed his arms, keeping his eyes from meeting hers as they waited for the nurse to come in. Once she did and the release documents were signed, Nash rose immediately and held open the door, as if he couldn't wait to get out of there. But as they made their way out to the parking lot, he still didn't speak.

When he reached for the passenger door handle, Bailey touched his shoulder. "Nash, say something."

He paused and closed his eyes, as if it pained him to speak. "I can't. Nothing I say will change a damn thing." He pulled open the door for her, then paced around to the driver's side, climbing behind the wheel.

Bailey winced, but tried not to take his gruff tone personally. He was angry and hurt. She understood that. Hell, she was upset, too. She was still having a hard time believing any of this had happened.

Maybe they both just needed some time to come to terms with it. Talking about it now while their emotions were running high and ricocheting all over the place wouldn't benefit anyone. There would be plenty of time to figure things out once the shock wore off.

But as she slid into the truck's cab, heated to a suffocating degree by the midday sun, she couldn't help but notice the chill in the air emanating from her husband. His expression held no emotion, no feeling. Just emptiness.

Had all of this been for nothing?

No. She didn't believe that. Not after she'd allowed herself to fall in love—

The thought struck her with such force, she gripped the edge of the seat to keep her body from pitching forward. She loved him? *Oh God! She did!* She'd gone and done the one thing she'd set out to avoid from the beginning.

I fell in love with my husband.

Head lowered, Nash gripped the steering wheel with both hands until his knuckles turned white. "I'm sorry," he said in a hushed tone. "I didn't mean to take it out on you. I don't know how to express what I'm feeling right now. I was just getting used to the idea of being a…" His words cut off and he shook his head, as if he were still in denial.

Bailey's heart broke for him.

She knew how much he'd wanted the baby from the beginning and had no doubt he would have been an amazing dad. Nash had always been the steadfast and strong one, so seeing him like this gnawed at her very soul.

She didn't want to push him. When he was ready and able to talk about it, he would. Until then, the only thing she could do was deal with her own feelings of loss in private to keep from adding to his agony and wait for him to open up. Then she'd be there for him. If he needed her to be the resilient one right now, then that was exactly what she'd be…for *him*.

Because she loved him.

Also because she refused to believe that the one thing that brought them together would be the one thing that would tear them apart. She couldn't lose him now. Not when she'd already invested her heart. They would get through this and come out stronger for it. They had to.

And she would make damn sure of it.

CHAPTER TWENTY-FOUR

WITHOUT TURNING ON any lights, Nash eased the bedroom door open and entered the room. Once his eyes adjusted to the dark, he quietly kicked off his boots, setting them down lightly to keep from disturbing Bailey, then stripped out of his shirt and tie.

She sat up in bed and rubbed her eyes. "Nash, is that you?"

"Yeah, it's me." He peeled off his slacks, which left him standing there in only his boxer-briefs. "Go back to sleep."

"Where have you been?"

Damn it. Here we go again. "I worked late," he said, trying to keep his annoyance in check. "I told you I wasn't going to be home for dinner."

"Yes, but it's almost midnight. I was worried."

He cringed, guilt eating at his conscience with a sharp fork. "Sorry. I should've called. I just had…things to take care of at the office."

Her silence reeked of confusion and irritation, but he didn't want to tell her he'd been meeting with the medical malpractice attorney in charge of handling the three—*soon to be four*—malpractice suits for the moronic doctor who'd given Bailey false test results.

It'd been two weeks since Dr. Stevenson had given them the news that Bailey wasn't pregnant, and he hadn't seen her cry once since leaving the hospital. It was like she was in denial or something. The moment they'd arrived home, she'd resumed her life, as if nothing had happened.

He'd expected her to have a mental breakdown. Especially after uprooting her entire life to marry a complete stranger, all so they could raise a child together…a child who didn't even exist. But she hadn't.

Instead, she cooked, cleaned the house, painted her toenails, watched that stupid soap opera he'd turned her onto, and had even taken up a fondness for bubble baths. He just didn't get it. Why was she acting so strange?

Hell, maybe she was still in shock. Lord knows, it had taken him a few hours to get his head screwed back on straight after hearing there was no baby. But by the time he'd worked through his own feelings, Bailey had planted a stoic expression on her face and asked him what he wanted for dinner, as if they hadn't just been given the worst news possible.

After three days of the same behavior, Nash finally consulted a psychologist who agreed Bailey's actions were consistent with someone who refused to accept the loss they'd suffered. Then she'd issued Nash a warning. The shrink had compared Bailey's actions to that of sleepwalking and said forcing his wife to come to terms with her grief before she was ready might do her more harm than good.

So instead, Nash set out to do the only thing he could. Take the bastard doctor who'd misdiagnosed Bailey to court and get his medical license stripped from his ass permanently. Only he couldn't mention it to Bailey. At least not yet.

Once she accepted she wasn't pregnant and worked through the fog of mourning that would accompany such a realization, only then would he show her the solid case he was building against the asshole doctor. Until then, he'd have to keep quiet.

"Nash, are we…okay?" Her voice crumbled.

"Hey," Nash said, sliding into the bed next to her. He cupped the back of her neck and stared straight into her moonlit eyes. "We're fine. It's just that I…"

Damn it. He couldn't tell her. Not fucking yet.

But the look on her face gutted him. He had to do something to erase the worry from her eyes and calm her fears. "Come here." He pulled her into his lap, wrapped his arms around her, and buried his face into her coconut-scented hair. "Everything is fine. I swear."

She held herself rigid in his arms, as if she could sense he was lying to her. Then she pulled back and frowned, burning him with dark eyes that begged him to tell her the truth. "Nash, please…"

I'm sorry, baby. I can't.

So he did the only thing he could do. He kissed her.

He only meant to comfort her—possibly even distract her a little—but the moment he fastened his mouth over hers, a familiar longing moved through him. It was like coming home again. God, he missed touching her like this.

Clad in only panties and a tight halter top, her plump lips parted timidly and his tongue swept inside to tangle with hers. She pressed her soft body into his and shivered, her nipples puckering against his chest.

Feeling the fervor of her response, Nash's cock hardened beneath her, surging upward, prodding at the barrier of her clothing. Had she been naked, his dick would have slipped into her with ease. *Fuck.*

Was it too soon? Would she think about the baby? The last he wanted to do was upset her or force the realization on her. Maybe he should stop before things went too far.

He broke the kiss and gently set her away from him. Restraint in the bedroom was never something he'd had much of when it came to her, but he would rather gouge his eyes out with a hot poker than do anything that might hinder her healing process.

But Bailey didn't seem at all pleased with the maneuver. The corners of her mouth drooped and wary eyes flickered over him, as if she took the rejection personally.

Without a word, she reached out and pulled down the front of his boxer-briefs, freeing his rock-hard dick. "Since *this* obviously isn't the problem, why don't you tell me what is? Why do you keep pushing me away?"

Sonofabitch. That wasn't what he was doing. He wanted to tell her he was trying to help her, that he was doing what was best *for* her. But damn it, he couldn't. "I'm tired, okay? Let's just go to bed—"

Without warning, she fisted his dick.

Oh God. Nash bit the inside of his cheek. "Bailey…"

Instead of answering him, she dropped her firm lips over his hot flesh, sucking vigorously. *Fuck.* He closed his eyes, reveling in the sensation, but didn't dare move. His control was already slipping and any motion on his part would only encourage him to do what he truly wanted, which was to yank those black panties down her legs and plunder her with various parts of his anatomy.

He resisted the desire to tangle his fingers in her silky hair, fought the urge to thrust upward into her velvety mouth, denied the impulse to flip her over and shove his dick where he wanted it most. But when she dragged her lips to the base of his shaft, allowing the head of his cock to rest snugly against the warm, fleshy part of her throat, and then swallowed around it, he knew he was screwed.

All control flew out the window.

Grasping her by the arms, Nash hauled Bailey up his body until she straddled his waist, and then gripped her hips roughly, grinding her against his aching length. He jerked the halter top over her head and tossed it aside. Then his insistent hands were on her, covering her breasts, while gently rolling her distended nubs between his fingertips.

She moaned and arched her back, thrusting her chest out even more, and he couldn't stop himself. His tongue darted out, bathing her nipples with long strokes of pleasure, while his hand traveled farther south.

His finger hooked into her panties, pulling them to the side, before positioning himself against her wet heat. She squirmed over him, as if waiting for him to thrust up inside her, but he didn't. Instead, he dug his fingers into her waist and grunted as he pulled her down hard onto his cock.

She moaned so deeply, he felt the vibration inside her.

His hand moved, caressing over her smooth skin until he found her. His fingers scissored around her clit, squeezing with just the right amount of pressure. Her inner muscles molded around him, clamping down on him, and her hips involuntarily flexed. Then she whimpered.

Leaning forward, he claimed her mouth once again. His erection swelled as she began to grind with purpose, undulating her pelvis slowly in a mind-blowing rhythm that was as torturous as it was pleasurable. He groaned, then grunted in frustration as he strained to hold himself still and let her have control, riding him at her own pace.

But when she sighed against his lips, the breathy sound ignited a fever in him that couldn't be restrained. Desire burned through him, fueling him to take her hard and fast. God, he wanted her. Wanted to feel her writhing beneath him as she came around his dick. And he needed to feel it right now.

Not bothering to pull out, he grasped her ass and rolled them over until she was flat on her back. She squeaked at the unexpected maneuver, but as he spread her legs farther apart and thrust deeper and harder than before, the sound turned into a moan. She arched her body upward, thrusting those pert little breasts into his face.

Nash closed his lips around one tight rosy nub, rasping his tongue across it as her body quivered in excitement. Her slick channel convulsed around him, warning of her impending climax. The moment she cried out her release, he pushed all the way inside her and held himself there, letting her contractions milk the orgasm from him. Grunting and groaning, he threw his head back and let go.

Depleted of all strength, he sank on top of her, instinctively angling his body to the side to keep from smothering her. "Jesus. You okay?"

"Mmm-hmm," she answered, her hands roaming over his back as she lovingly caressed him. "Aren't you?"

Nash blew out a breath. "I'm good."

"Good, because I need to tell you something." She played with his hair, combing her fingers through it. "I got my old job back at the restaurant."

Nash shot straight up. "What the hell are you talking about? Since when?"

She paused, seemingly confused by his outburst. "Since this morning. I called to give them my forwarding address, and Danny offered to put me back on the schedule. I start my first shift tomorrow."

"No. Absolutely not." He crawled out of the bed, adjusted his underwear, flipped on the nearest light, and crossed his arms. There was no fucking way he was going to let her go back to work when she still hadn't accepted she was no longer pregnant. "You aren't going back to work."

"Why not?"

He couldn't tell her why, but he had to give her a good reason. Something believable. Something to keep her from taking the job. "Because I'm your husband and I said so, that's why." *Oh, fuck. Where the hell did that come from?* The moment the words left his lips, he knew it was the wrong thing to say.

She blinked in shock, then her eyes flared with anger. "Excuse me?" She scoffed under her breath. "If you think that macho bullshit will fly with me, then you married the wrong girl."

Damn it. Now he had to tell her the truth to keep her from being pissed at him. But not knowing how she would react weighed heavily on his shoulders. "Bailey, just let me explain—"

"I don't want to hear it, Nash. I married you, but you are not my keeper. I'm a grown woman who'll make her own decisions, and if you don't like it, then that's just too damn bad. I wasn't asking your permission. I was politely informing you of my plans. But I won't have you telling me what I can or can't—"

"Goddamnit, Bailey. Just shut up and listen."

She flinched, as if he'd struck her, and the cool gaze she shot his way sent chills down his spine. Before he could even apologize, she rose from the bed and calmly walked out of the bedroom, wearing nothing but her panties and slamming the door behind her.

Fucking great.

CHAPTER TWENTY-FIVE

BAILEY COULDN'T WAIT for her shift to end.

Not only were her feet killing her, but she was exhausted and unable to concentrate. No doubt it had to do with the miserable, sleepless nights she'd spent in the guest room after her argument with Nash. It'd been three days since she'd spoken a word to him. *That'll teach him to tell me to shut up.*

But the silent treatment was getting to her, too.

That first night, he'd tried to apologize, but she'd been so pissed that she'd locked the guest room door and ignored his pleas for her to open it. Even when he gave up and went back into the other room, neither of them had gotten much sleep. She'd heard him pacing in the room next to hers, then listened to the creaking of the bed as he tossed and turned almost as much as she had.

The next day, they'd avoided one another altogether. She'd started back at her old job, apparently against his wishes, while Nash had worked late into the night once again. Even though she'd left the guest room door unlocked that night, he'd passed right by it and never bothered to knock or open it. Bailey had cried softly for an hour, then spent the rest of the night staring at the ceiling.

But last night had been the worst of all. They'd sat at the kitchen table, eating dinner in complete silence. A couple of times, he'd looked like he wanted to say something, but hadn't. So she did the same thing she'd been doing every night since the doctor told her she wasn't pregnant. She went into the bathroom, turned on the water in the bathtub, and had cried until her tears ran dry, letting the sound of the running water drown out her sadness.

She couldn't understand how they had been so happy, and then in one instant, their relationship had become stagnant and their marriage had taken a nosedive. But then again, this had never been a real marriage from the beginning. Not really. She had been a vessel, an incubator for his unborn child. At least, that's what he'd believed when he'd married her. Now that it was no longer the case, maybe this was his way of telling her he wanted out of the marriage.

The thought alone stressed her out, so she shook it off. She had enough on her plate at the moment and didn't want to think about it right now, anyway. She'd barely made it through the lunch rush without screwing up an order. All she wanted was to take her last customer's order and then get the hell out of there. Even if the thought of going home and facing Nash left her feeling anxious.

She headed for the lone man in the dark gray suit who'd unbuttoned his jacket before sitting at the nearby table the hostess had shown him to. Occasionally businessmen came into Danny's establishment, but this particular one seemed severely out of place. As if he had an air of sophistication or entitlement about him and wouldn't normally be caught dead in a bar and grill.

"Hi, I'm Bailey," she said with a smile. "I'll be your server today. What can I get you to drink?"

He glanced up at her and one haughty brow rose before he gestured to the chair across from him. "Actually, I'd like a word with you, Ms. Hobbs. Or do you prefer I call you Mrs. Sutherland?"

Bailey hesitated. Though there was something awfully familiar about him, she'd never given out her last name to a customer before. Not her maiden name, and definitely not her married one. But then he flashed her a superior grin, showing off his perfect pearly whites, and she had no doubt about his identity.

Only Nash had that same lady killer smile, one he'd obviously inherited from his estranged father. "Does your son know you're here?"

That earned her another quick smile. "No, I don't believe he does."

Bailey sat in the seat across from him and folded her hands on the table in front of her. "Do you plan on telling him?"

"Well, at the moment, my son isn't speaking to me."

"I'm sure he has his reasons."

"Ah, yes, I suppose he does." Aaron Sutherland leaned back in his chair, measuring her with his eyes. "Which is exactly why I came to see you."

Her brows lowered over her wary eyes. "What does any of this have to do with me?"

"Well, it's quite simple, really. I'd like Nash to take the position I offered him as the head of the legal department for Sutherland Industries, but he's as stubborn as his mother. He just won't listen to reason. But as his wife, *you* could make that happen."

"I'm not going to ask Nash to take the job."

He chuckled at her. "That's not what I'm proposing."

"Then maybe you should just spell it out for me," she told him, trying to keep her tone even and failing miserably. "What exactly do you want from me, Mr. Sutherland?"

"I want you to persuade my son to talk to me, to hear me out. And I'm willing to make it worth your while." Nash's father pulled a check from his pocket and slid it across the table toward her.

She didn't even bother to look at it. "No."

"If it's not enough of an incentive, I'm happy to make you a better offer."

"I said no."

Determination darkened his eyes with a controlled intensity. Like Nash, Aaron Sutherland didn't like to be told no. But that was just too damn bad. She was on her husband's side, and if his dad didn't understand that, then the selfish bastard didn't know the first meaning of love.

"I don't think I'm making myself clear. I'm willing to pay you a considerable sum for your cooperation. But you only have ten seconds before I withdraw my proposal."

"I don't think I'm making myself clear," she said, glaring at him. "I said no."

"Maybe I should explain it a different way." Nash's father adjusted his sleeve and then pointed with the gold cuff link at his wrist, monogrammed with the letters *A* and *S*. "Do you know what I pay for these alone?"

"Apparently more than you should have." Bailey leaned forward and shoved the check back to him. "But you don't have enough money in the bank to buy me off. If you want Nash to listen to you, then maybe you should learn to do the same." She stood up to leave, but stopped long enough to glance back at his custom-made cuff link. "By the way, you're missing a letter. After meeting you in person, I am certain there should be another *S* at the end." Then she marched away.

Bailey stayed in the back room until she was sure he'd left. Then she clocked out and headed home. She couldn't believe Nash's father would stoop so low. *The nerve!* No wonder her husband wanted nothing to do with him. Aaron Sutherland was an egotistical prick who thought his money and power could buy him anything he wanted...including his own son.

He hadn't said he missed Nash, or even loved him. Only that he wanted his son to take his position in the family business. In fact, he didn't seem to care at all about what Nash wanted. Because as long as Aaron got his way, that was all that mattered.

Bailey sighed.

She felt terrible that she and Nash weren't on speaking terms because all she wanted to do right now was wrap her arms around his waist and tell him how much she loved him. Screw their argument. Forget waiting for him to get past the hurt of losing a child that was never meant to be. It was time he knew how she felt. And she planned to tell him tonight, the moment he walked through the front door.

Fifteen minutes later, Bailey pulled into the driveway of her home and got a pleasant surprise. Nash's truck was already parked out front in his usual spot. She smiled. Maybe he was here to fix things with her as well. God, she hoped so.

She hurried inside and spotted him almost immediately. He stood in the kitchen doorway, staring silently at her, as if he were waiting for her to get home. "I'm glad you're here," she told him. "We need to talk."

"Yes, we do," he agreed, though his voice sounded a little off. "How was work?"

Bailey shrugged. "It was okay."

"Just okay?" His eyebrow rose slightly. "Why? Did something happen?"

ALISON BLISS

"No, nothing." Guilt punched her in the gut, and she cringed internally. She didn't like lying to her husband, but there was no point in hurting him by confirming something he already knew: his father was a pompous asshole.

He regarded her with wary eyes. "Are you sure? You look like something is bothering you."

"I'm fine. I just don't like it when we fight." She reached for him, wanting to coil her arms around his waist, but he grasped her arms to stop her. The potent smell of alcohol assaulted her nostrils, and one glance at the half empty bottle on the table confirmed her suspicions. He reeked of whiskey. "Have you been drinking?"

"Yeah." He released her arms and stepped back from her.

He must still be mad. "Look, I'm sorry. I just wanted—" He looked away from her, fists clenching at his sides, but didn't say anything. "Nash...? What's wrong?"

A moment passed before he spoke. "I'm trying to figure out what you're apologizing for." The way he regarded her with a hard gaze concerned her, but it was the remoteness in his gruff voice that alarmed her the most. "Are you sorry about the fight...or that you lied to me again?"

"What are you talking about?"

"I'm talking about your inability to tell me the fucking truth," he snapped, making her eyes widen. He pursed his lips briefly. "Then again, I guess you've done nothing but lie to me from the beginning, anyway."

"Nash, I don't know what it is you think I lied to you about—"

"Bailey. Stop it!" His dark eyes wielded an anger she'd never seen from him before. He paced back and forth like an aggravated panther in an unreliable cage. "I know, all right? Earlier, I went by the restaurant to put an end to our argument, and I saw you meeting with my dad."

Shit. "I can explain—"

He scowled at her. "Right. Because I can believe anything that comes out of your mouth?"

"Nash, just listen to me."

"Oh, I did. When you asked me to give my father another chance or fed me the bullshit guilt trip about how I'd regret not

166

talking to him if something ever happened to him." He shook his head. "No, thanks. I'm done listening to you."

"Nash, that meeting with your dad wasn't what it looked like."

"Oh, yeah? Then explain this." He swiped a folded newspaper off the counter and thrust it at her. "Look familiar?"

"It's...my newspaper. So what?"

Nash groaned. "Don't act stupid, Bailey."

"Me? You're the one playing guessing games. Why don't you just tell me what this newspaper has to do with anything?"

He snatched the paper from her hand, flipped it over, and tapped his finger on the article on the other side that read NEW HEAD OF LEGAL DEPARTMENT FOR SUTHERLAND INDUSTRIES. "This. You've been in cahoots with my father from the beginning, haven't you?"

"What? Why would you even think that? Damn it, Nash. The only reason I held onto this newspaper was because, when I was on bedrest, I didn't finish the crossword puzzle on the back. Today was the first time I've ever met your dad. He showed up at my work and asked me to help him by getting you to talk to him. I refused."

"Bullshit," Nash yelled, throwing the newspaper on the floor. "I watched him push a check across the table to you, but what I didn't see was you bothering to rip it in half. So what was I worth to you, Bailey? How much money did my dad pay you to marry me and fuck me over?"

Tears stung her eyes, and she shook her head. She'd never seen him so angry, but it all boiled down to one thing. "You really don't trust me at all, do you?"

"Why should I? Since the first day I met you, everything that has come out of your mouth has been a lie. Hell, I'd be shocked if your mother was actually dead."

Speechless, Bailey reeled back, and her hand flew to her chest. How could he say something so cruel? The gut-wrenching pain of his callous words infuriated her, but she managed to restrain the urge to slap him. Barely.

Instead, she turned on her heel, stormed into the bedroom, and began packing her things. He'd given her no choice. Her own husband couldn't give her the very thing he'd asked of her on their wedding night—*trust*—so there wasn't much of a point in trying to save a marriage that had been doomed from the beginning.

As she placed her belongings in her suitcase, a constant drip of tears leaked down her face, but she was powerless to stop them. With each item of clothing she packed, her stomach twisted more and a stabbing pain invaded her heart, ripping it to shreds. When she couldn't stand it anymore, she gave up and zipped her suitcase closed. She couldn't bear to stay in that house for another second knowing she'd lost the only man she ever truly loved. He could sell the rest of her things like he'd done once before.

As she wheeled her suitcase toward the front door, she caught a glimpse of Nash standing in the kitchen, pouring himself another drink. He didn't even bother to look up. Why did things have to turn out this way? Why did loving someone hurt so much?

She put her hand on the knob, but heard his footsteps approach from behind her. "Where the hell do you think you're going?"

"I'm leaving."

Nash shook his head angrily. "Bullshit. We're married. You can't just walk out on me."

"Watch me. I can't be with someone who doesn't trust me." Then she looked directly at him to make sure he didn't miss the conviction of her words. "It's over."

Fire flashed in his eyes. "Bailey, I'm warning you. If you walk out that door, I won't come after you."

She lifted her chin. "Good. I don't want you to."

Then she left.

CHAPTER TWENTY-SIX

NASH WOKE UP miserable, hungover, and even more pissed off than when he'd passed out. He couldn't believe Bailey had walked out on him last night. Or that he'd resorted to sleeping in the guest room because it was the only bed where her scent still lingered on the fucking sheets.

Damn it.

His head pounded, but it had nothing on the way his heart battered the hell out of his rib cage. He rubbed at the unshaven stubble on his face. He looked and felt like hell, but the last thing he planned to do was sit around wallowing in self-pity. He hadn't been capable of driving anywhere last night, but he had someone he needed to pay a visit to.

And it wasn't the wife who'd left him.

He headed into the kitchen to make a pot of coffee, but stopped when he saw the newspaper laying in the middle of the floor. He snatched it up and started to toss it on the counter when he saw the half-completed crossword puzzle on the back. He glared at it for a second and then threw it down.

Didn't mean a fucking thing. Not after what he'd witnessed yesterday.

He'd gone to the bar and grill to make up with her, but through the front windows of the restaurant, Nash had caught a glimpse of his father sitting at one of the tables...with Bailey. He couldn't hear what they were saying, but his father was grinning relentlessly as he pulled a check from his suit pocket and placed it in front of her.

But even then, Nash had given her the benefit of doubt. Breath held, he'd waited for her to balk at the monetary gesture, rip the check to pieces, or simply get up and leave. But she hadn't. Instead, she'd appeared calm and unfazed as she kept her ass planted in the chair across from his dad. Hell, she never even glanced down at the check before her...as if she knew exactly how much that bastard had paid her.

That's when Nash had high-tailed it out of there in a full-on bout of rage. He would have confronted them both right then, but he'd been afraid of what he might do to his father if he stepped into the same room with the man.

And then there was Bailey.

While he'd waited for her to get home from work, he'd talked himself into giving her one last chance to tell him the truth. For a brief moment, he'd let himself hope she would do so. But now he regretted that decision. She'd looked him square in the eyes and lied to his face...again. Without so much as flinching. *Damn her.*

Yesterday, he'd made the decision to walk away without confronting his father in hopes of saving his marriage. But the moment Bailey walked out that door, Nash had nothing else to lose. He shook his head. "Fuck it."

By the time he changed his clothes and flung himself into his truck, he was fully worked up and ready to face the one person who deserved the lashing he was about to dish out.

His father.

Nash drove into Houston and headed straight to Sutherland Industries. When he arrived, he didn't bother to slow down long enough for the secretary to announce him. He barged right into his dad's office to find his father sitting at his pristine cherry oak desk with his right ankle kicked up over his left knee. His fingers were linked behind his head and the man looked entirely too comfortable in his fancy office.

But Nash was about to put an end to that.

He marched over to stand in front of the man who spent his life bullying his only child. "You're a lousy, self-righteous prick!"

"Now, son, is that any way to talk to your old man?"

"How much was I worth, huh? What's the going price for my wife to get me to have a conversation with you? Twenty thousand? Fifty thousand?"

"Oh, please. Give me more credit than that. I never would have offered her less than six figures."

Nash's jaw tightened. "Well, no wonder she left me so quickly." His mind rewound to the hurt look on Bailey's face when she'd walked out the door. "You must've given her a bonus for that stellar performance."

"Son, I hate to tell you this, but I don't have a clue as to what you're talking about. She left you?"

"Wasn't that part of your deal? You've been secretly meeting with her behind my back. I'm sure the subject of our marriage status came up."

"Nash, I didn't meet your wife until yesterday when I paid her a visit at that dingy restaurant. And we never had a deal. She didn't take the money I offered her. Actually, she turned me down flat and then called me an ass." His father couldn't contain his grin. "I like her."

"Don't bullshit me. You paid her off, and she hauled ass."

His father leaned farther back in his chair. "What the hell would I get out of asking her to leave you? I was trying to get her to talk to you on my behalf. She can't very well do that if she isn't with you, now can she?"

He stared at the man in front of him, measuring him with his eyes and gauging his sincerity. "Christ." His father wasn't lying. He might be a pretentious bastard who tried to force his son into doing what he wanted, but he'd never been much of a liar. "Shit. I need to borrow your phone."

"Why?"

"Because after the things I said to her, Bailey probably won't answer her phone if she thinks I'm the one calling."

His father leaned over the desk and pushed the phone toward Nash, who yanked up the receiver and quickly dialed Bailey's cell phone number. It rang three times before she finally answered. "Hello?"

"Bailey, don't hang up." There was a dead pause on the other end of the line. "I need to talk to you."

"No."

He rubbed at his face as his dad looked on. "Come on, Bailey. Let me explain."

"Definitely not." Her voice was curt.

"Look, I know you didn't take the money my dad offered you. My father said—"

"I don't give a damn what your father said." She breathed out, then sniffled into the line, making Nash cringe with regret. "You should have trusted me. But you didn't. So there's nothing left to talk about."

"You're right. I should have trusted you. I'm sorry I didn't. I need to see you in person and make this right. Please tell me where you are."

"That's none of your business."

"Damn it, Bailey, you're my wife."

"Not for much longer," she said, her weak voice warbling slightly, hinting at the heartbreak she felt. "I...I want a divorce."

No! Panic slammed into his chest, making it harder to breathe. He couldn't let that happen. *No fucking way.* Even if she didn't feel the same way, Bailey needed to know what she meant to him, what she was walking away from. He loved her. And he needed to find her. Now. "Goddamnit. Where are you?"

The line went dead.

"Damn it." Nash hit redial several times, but her phone went straight to voicemail. "Fuck!" He leaned on the desk and heaved out a hard breath, trying to figure out what to do.

"If you want my advice—"

"I don't. You've done enough already." He ran his hand over his face. "I just need to find her."

"It's one woman. How hard could it be?"

Nash rolled his eyes. "You wouldn't believe me if I told you."

"Try me."

"It took me a month to find her before...and that was with her staying in one place. I don't even know which state she's in. By now, she's probably somewhere between here and Alaska."

"Alaska, huh?" His dad didn't look the least bit surprised.

"You did a background check on her, didn't you?"

"Of course I did. You think I'd let my only son marry someone without making sure they weren't some kind of con artist? I checked out her father, too. And I must say, he was not an easy man to find."

Sonofabitch. If Bailey made it to Alaska before Nash could stop her, it would take him months to find her. He didn't have the endless resources his dad had access to, including Sutherland Industries' team of private investigators. Nash had invested all of his inheritance into building a life Aaron Sutherland couldn't control.

"Nash, she loves you. That was apparent the moment she turned down my offer. But I'm warning you, if you don't go to her soon, you're going to lose her. I should know. Your mother loved me, but by the time I realized I had lost her, it was already too late for us. She moved on…without me. Don't make the same damn mistake I did."

Nash blinked at his father. He'd never heard him say anything like that before. In fact, he had always gotten the impression that his father couldn't care less that his mom had left him. Guess his dad wasn't invincible, after all. Maybe the old man was finally coming around and making a change for the better. "I can't go to her. She won't tell me where she is."

"Son, you're a Sutherland. Make her tell you."

"Yeah, because that worked out so well for you with Mom? The more you tried to roll over her, the more your relationship deteriorated—"

Aw, hell. Is that what I've been doing to Bailey all along? From the beginning, he'd asked her to trust him, but he hadn't given her the same respect. Not really.

From the first moment he thought she had been pregnant with his child, he hadn't considered her feelings in the decisions that needed to be made. He'd just made them and expected her to go along with it. Hell, he'd even pushed her into marrying him, treating her like some prized trophy, rather than an equal lifelong partner.

Jesus. He was more like his father than he'd ever imagined. "I…I need to find her."

His old man shrugged and leaned back in his chair. "I could help you, you know?" A wry grin tugged at his mouth.

"At what price?"

"Well, I hear we're looking for a new head in our legal department. I could put in a good word for you."

So much for making a change, the arrogant asshole.

It was just as Nash thought. His dad never let a golden opportunity slip between his fingers. Aaron Sutherland looked at everything as a business venture, and it was a perfect chance to force his only son into working in the family business. Nash had played right into his hands.

But he'd do anything to find Bailey and bring her back home where she belonged. Even if that meant taking a job he didn't want and working for a man he loathed.

Fuck his pride. He just wanted his wife back.

"Done. Now help me find her."

CHAPTER TWENTY-SEVEN

BAILEY'S HEAD POUNDED relentlessly.

Her bruised sternum and tender abdomen were worrisome, but they didn't hurt her nearly as much as hearing Nash's voice on the phone had. So what if he admitted he should've trusted her—that didn't mean he *did* trust her. And she couldn't be with someone who wouldn't give her the same thing he'd asked of her. She deserved better than that, didn't she?

She shifted in her hospital bed, trying to get comfortable. An impossible task with all the cuts and contusions she'd received in the accident earlier that morning. She'd just quit her job at the bar and grill—for the last time—when an old lady driving an older model sedan veered out of her own lane and into Bailey's lane.

After that, everything had happened in slow motion. She'd hit the brakes and tried to swerve in time, but the two vehicles collided head on. The windshield shattered and glass rained inside the car as the airbag detonated and her body jerked against the seatbelt. She hadn't felt any pain at the time, but now that her adrenaline had settled and she was past her shocked state, whiplash was paying her a visit.

If only the elderly woman had restrained her dog in some way, none of this would have happened. But no. Instead, she'd left the dog loose in the front seat and the pooch had jumped into its owner's lap with no warning, causing the accident.

Cuts and bruises had been the worst of it for both of the drivers involved, but it could have turned out very differently. And that's what scared the hell out of Bailey. What if she had died? Would Nash know she loved him?

Even though she'd told him she wanted a divorce yesterday, his face was the one that flashed in her mind when the accident had occurred. She couldn't bear the thought of never seeing him again. She loved him. He obviously didn't return the sentiment, though. If he did, he would have put the same amount of trust in her as she had in him.

Now what the hell was she supposed to do?

She couldn't leave. That was no longer an option. Too much had happened between them and she owed it to Nash to tell him the truth. But would he ever offer her the trust she'd given to him? Or would it always be one-sided?

When someone burst through the door, Bailey jumped and her head swung toward the sound. Nash stood in the doorway, looking haggard and disheveled while breathing heavily, as if he'd run every corridor in the hospital searching for her. His bloodshot eyes were wide and worried, but he didn't speak. He rushed to her side and crawled halfway into the bed with her, gently wrapping his familiar arms around her. "I'm so sorry about everything. I thought... Jesus."

She sagged against his chest, feeling him pull in a ragged breath. "Nash?"

"Baby, I thought I lost you for good. When I was told you had been in an accident, I...I couldn't get here fast enough. I thought I was too late."

"I'm okay. Just some minor injuries." She breathed in, relishing in his scent. God, she missed being in his arms like this. "How did you find me?"

"My father."

She pulled back to gaze at him. "Your father? Why would he help you find me after the way he treated both of us?"

"Because I finally gave him what he wanted." His nostrils flared.

"Nash, no! Please tell me you didn't take the position."

He shrugged lightly, as if none of it mattered. "It's just a job. Besides, it was worth it to know you're okay. You scared the hell out of me." He cupped her head and kissed her on the lips, letting his mouth linger over hers. "I'm sorry. I should have told you this a long time ago, but I love you, Bailey. I'm so in love with you I can't see straight."

Tears pricked her eyes, but she held them back. There were so many things she wanted to say to him. "I love you, too."

"Baby, I need you. Please tell me you'll come home with me and let me make it up to you."

"Nash…" She lowered her head. "I can't until—"

"Sweetheart, I know what a jackass I was. I should have believed you, trusted you to tell me the truth. I've never had anyone stand up to my father for me like you did." He grasped her hand and held it tight as his eyes fastened to hers. "I know what I lost when you walked out that door, and I don't ever want to feel that way again. After everything we've been through, I can't lose you now. I want you. God, I need you in my life. Please say you'll come home with me."

"I have something I need to tell you first."

"Okay, I'm listening."

She grinned at him. "I'm pregnant."

He stared at her, without blinking. "How? I mean, I know *how*, but…are you sure?"

"When I was admitted, the doctor asked me if there were any chance I was pregnant. I told him no, but he ordered blood tests, anyway."

"Wait. You knew you weren't pregnant? You acted so normal after we returned home that day after being told there wasn't a baby. I thought you hadn't accepted it."

"I knew. I was just trying to be strong…for you. I could see you were having a hard time dealing with the loss of our child, so I didn't want to burden you—"

"Sweetheart, you couldn't burden me if you tried." He leaned over and kissed her forehead, then placed his warm hand on her belly. "But you're really pregnant this time?"

She grinned. "They confirmed it with a sonogram. I'm definitely pregnant."

"And the baby is okay? After the accident, I mean?"

"Yes, the doctor said everything was fine. I just can't wait to get out of here."

"You ready to come home and finish what we started?"

Bailey wrapped her arms around his neck and kissed him hard. "I wouldn't want to be anywhere else."

FOUR MONTHS LATER, Bailey pulled up at Sutherland Industries and made her way to her father-in-law's office. She didn't wait for the secretary's approval. Instead, Bailey marched past the woman's desk and shoved open his door without knocking.

Nash stood in his dad's office and froze when he saw her. "Bailey? How did you know I was in here going over a case?"

"I didn't." Bailey kept her eyes firmly glued to Aaron, who was sitting on the edge of his desk looking over Nash's shoulder. "I came to speak with your dad."

Both men exchanged looks, but Aaron grinned. "Nash, why don't you give me a few minutes alone with your lovely wife?"

"Bailey...?" Nash asked, raising a brow.

"It's fine. It's about time your father and I got a few things straightened out."

Nash hesitated. "Are you sure?"

"Yes," she replied. "It'll just take a moment of his time. I'm sure a man of such importance can spare that for his daughter-in-law."

Nash nodded at her and stepped out of the room without another word, pulling the door closed behind him. He really did trust her, after all.

"Would you like something to drink?" Aaron asked.

"No, thank you. I'd rather just say what I came to say, if that's okay with you."

Nash's dad gazed at her warily. "What can I do for you, Mrs. Sutherland?"

"You can fire my husband and let him go back to his practice. He's been killing himself for months trying to do both jobs, and I've had enough."

Aaron shook his head. "I can't do that. I'm sorry. Nash is a great lawyer and he's an asset to Sutherland Industries." He looked a little confused, though. "I didn't know he was still running his own practice on the side. Why would he do that?"

178

"Because unlike you, he's an honorable man. Nash didn't want to leave his clients in a lurch and run out on them. It was bad enough he spent the last few months focusing all his extra time on the malpractice suit in order to put that quack doctor out of business for good. Now that we've won our case in court, there's only one thing keeping Nash from going back to his own practice. But he made you a deal and he refuses to bail out on the position you forced him into. So *I'm* telling you. Let him go."

"And why the hell would I do that?"

"You already lost your wife due to your overbearing ways. If you keep Nash on and force him to continue working for you, you will lose him too. The only things you have left are these grandchildren of yours I'm carrying."

"Grandchildren? You mean—"

"Yep, twins. We found out yesterday. A boy and a girl."

Aaron wrinkled his brow. "I've been with Nash all morning, and…he never even mentioned the possibility of two babies."

"Do you blame him?"

"Well, no, I guess not. But what do the babies have to do with—"

"*Your* grandchild may be Sutherlands, but guess who's holding the key to that golden gate?" She raised a brow. "Yep, that's right. You have to go through me. And if you think I'm going to let you bully *my* children into anything, you're dead wrong."

Nash's father blinked in shock. "So this is your way of saying you're planning to hold my grandchildren over my head?"

Bailey smiled, knowing she had hit her target. "Damn straight. Your wife has already divorced you. Your relationship with your son is fragile at best. And these babies are the last Sutherlands who may want anything to do with you in the future. But there's only one way that is ever going to happen. It's your decision."

He thought about that for a moment. "How soon do you need an answer?"

"Now. In fact, you only have ten seconds before I withdraw my proposal."

He scowled at her, but walked over and opened the office door to find Nash waiting on the other side. "You're fired," he said, then walked out of the office without looking back.

"What the...?" Nash shook his head at her. "Bailey, what did you do?"

She rubbed her hand over her swollen stomach. "Let's just say I gave your father some incentive to let you go and find a new head for his legal department."

Nash smiled at that. "You didn't have to do that. I don't care where I work as long as you're the one I'm coming home to."

She winked at him. "I'll be there. You can count on it."

He pulled her into his arms and kissed her long and hard. "I just never know what to expect out of you these days, Mrs. Sutherland."

"That's easy," she said, giggling. "Expect the unexpected."

ABOUT ALISON BLISS

ALISON BLISS GREW up in Small Town, Texas, but currently resides in the Midwest with her husband and two sons. With so much testosterone in her home, it's no wonder she writes "girl books." She believes the best way to know if someone is your soul mate is by canoeing with them because if you both make it back alive, it's obviously meant to be. Alison pens the type of books she loves to read most: fun, steamy love stories with heart, heat, laughter, and usually a cowboy or two. As she calls it, "Romance...with a sense of humor."

To learn more about Alison Bliss, visit her website at http://authoralisonbliss.com, where you can sign up for her newsletter to keep up with her latest book news. You can also email her at authoralisonbliss@hotmail.com or connect with her on social media.

Facebook: http://facebook.com/AuthorAlisonBliss
Twitter: http://twitter.com/AlisonBliss2
Goodreads: http://goodreads.com/AlisonBliss
Pinterest: http://pinterest.com/AlisonBliss2

ALSO BY ALISON BLISS

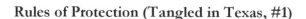

Rules of Protection (Tangled in Texas, #1)

Some rules are meant to be broken...

It's rule breaker Emily Foster's birthday, and like everyone at The Jungle Room, she just wants to get some action. Unfortunately, she stumbles on the wrong kind, witnessing a mob hit. To protect her, she's entered into the Witness Protection Program with by-the-book Special Agent Jake Ward as her chaperone.

When the location of their safe house is compromised, Jake stashes Emily deep in the Texas backwoods. The city-girl might be safe from the Mafia, but she has to contend with a psychotic rooster, a narcoleptic dog, crazy cowboys, and the danger of losing her heart to the one man she can't have.

Jake's as hot as he is infuriating, and she can't help but push all his buttons to loosen him up. Their mutual, sizzling sexual attraction poses a dilemma: Jake's determined to keep her safe and out of the wrong hands; she's determined to get into the right ones—his.

ALSO BY ALISON BLISS

Playing With Fire (Tangled in Texas, #2)

Nothing ignites a fire like the perfect match...

Anna Weber is every inch the proper librarian--old-fashioned, conservatively dressed right down to her tightly clipped flaming red hair. She's just moved to a small Texas town, and is determined to spend time with her friend before she has to disappear. Relationships aren't easy for her. She knows too well what it means to be burned. And the last thing she ever wants to do is fall in love...

Especially not with a fireman who's hot enough to set the entire state of Texas on fire.

Cowboy can't resist the fiery little librarian, and he's determined to make her *his*. Beneath that prim-and-proper exterior is a woman he very much wants to know--if she'd let him. She'll test his patience. His control. Hell, his very *sanity*. And for the first time, Cowboy wonders if he's found the one fire he can't control...

Made in United States
Orlando, FL
02 April 2023

31686441R00114